GH00865004

Sleeping ᴠ

"A delightful fairy story that deals sensᴜ...
compellingly with real, modern-day issues like
homelessness, single mums and abusive parents."
*George Layton, actor, screenwriter and author of bestsellers, 'The
Trick', 'The Swap' and 'The Fib'*

"Wonderful images and thought-provoking scenes."
*Bramwell Tovey, Grammy Award-winning composer, conductor
and broadcaster*

"The strength of the author's voice held me captivated long
after turning the last page. With the wit of JK Rowling,
Alex Pearl has definitely earned his place in the young
adult fiction hall of fame. His fantasy broaches the
subjects of homelessness, child adoption, bullying,
injustice, and the cruelty of abusive parents, all issues with
which the youth of today live. There is a moral lesson for
each of Pearl's characters to learn. Through a marvellous
turn of events, each character is rewarded with the right
ending. Bravo, Alex Pearl!"
Lisa McCombs for Readers' Favorite

"The story skips along at a lively pace, the characters are
lifelike and believable, and it manages to address
important issues such as poor parenting, bullying and
homelessness in an accessible, non-intimidating way. It
would make excellent bedtime reading and the climax in
particular is packed full of images which I can imagine
staying in a child's dreamy head for a long time."
*Chris Chalmers, award-winning author of 'Five to One' and the
highly acclaimed 'Light From Other Windows'*

First published in Great Britain by Pen Press in 2011
This edition published in 2015

A catalogue record of this book is available from the British Library
Cover photography by John Mac
Cover design and typography by Lyndon Povey
Typesetting by Red Button Publishing

Sleeping with the Blackbirds

ALEX PEARL

About the Author

This is Alex Pearl's first work of fiction. It was inspired by his 13-year-old son who has an affinity with birds and can, when pressed, produce an uncanny imitation of a seagull.

For over 25 years Alex has been employed by numerous advertising agencies as a copywriter.

Alex is married with two children and lives in North West London.

Contents

For Jennifer, Sarah and Jonathan. And in memory of
Avrom, a wonderful dad, grandpa and friend.

Hope is the thing with feathers

That perches in the soul,

And sings the tune without words,

And never stops at all.

Emily Dickinson

ONE

The Garden

The garden at number 44 Orchard Drive was a perfectly ordinary little garden. There was a small bumpy lawn with its fair share of dandelions and clover. There was an old rickety shed that leaned precariously among the stinging nettles. And then there were the trees: two apple trees, a cherry tree and a magnificent old oak with an enormous gnarled trunk and knobbly limbs that stretched skyward. It may not have seemed like a particularly special garden to the casual onlooker, but to Roy Nuttersley it was the perfect place. The perfect place at least to while away a few hours each day, to forget his troubles and escape the hurly-burly of everyday life.

This morning he'd woken up early and was peering through his bedroom window that looked out onto the little patch of tranquillity at the back of the house. He held the plastic binoculars that his granny had given him for his eleventh birthday to his eyes and brought the view into focus. His newly constructed bird feeders were still there swaying gently in the morning breeze. There were eight in total hanging from the branches of the two apple trees. He had designed and built them all himself and taken much time to paint them with the leftover paints his dad had stored in the shed. The birds had obviously appreciated his efforts, as they could now be seen darting here, there and everywhere, twittering in delight as they went.

Why, thought Roy, couldn't human beings go about their lives twittering joyfully like the little birds, rather than being grumpy all the time? Although he wasn't so sure that all parents were quite as nasty to each other as his were.

After all, he did see Samantha Bradbury's parents smiling at each other at the school gates last Wednesday. And he could have sworn he saw two grown-ups kissing on a bus once, and he was pretty sure they were married.

As a little blue tit popped his head out of a bright orange bird feeder, Roy could hear stirring noises coming from that other habitat nearby: his parents' bedroom. Roy's dad was a large man in every sense of the word. Stanley Nuttersley had a large balding head, a large bulbous nose and an incredibly large tummy. His overall shape resembled a larger than life skittle. This, thought Roy, was probably down to his dad's fondness for all things sugary and creamy; iced cream buns and liberally sugared doughnuts especially.

So it was hardly surprising that the bed should creak and groan as Stanley rolled over onto his side.

Angela Nuttersley, a rather small woman by comparison, with a turned up nose and squirrel-like features, woke up with a jolt.

"You've woken me up again you loathsome waste of skin," she bellowed at her husband.

Monday morning, it seemed, was about to begin.

TWO

The Family

"You nincompoop of a husband. Look where you've put the dinner plates. And why oh why have you left the washing in the washing machine you cretinous numbskull?" Angela Nuttersley may have been a relatively small woman, but what she lacked in stature she more than made up for with a fine set of vocal cords. She would moan, condemn, complain, and scold her husband relentlessly. And Stanley Nuttersley would seethe quietly like a large simmering volcano, until he could take his wife's verbal barrage no longer; at which point he'd explode.

"Don't be such a ridiculous little woman. Who on earth do you think does all the work around here?" His retaliation would always reverberate around the four walls of the small kitchen and cause the plates on the bottom shelf of the cupboard to rattle. At this stage of the proceedings, hostilities would escalate to such an extent that neither would notice that their son had dutifully eaten his cornflakes, washed up his bowl and let himself out of the front door to go to school.

A ceasefire would usually occur at around 8.30am when Mr Nuttersley would look at his watch, realize he was running late for work at his shirt factory and fly out of the front door while still munching a piece of toast with a thick coat of marmalade.

By this time Roy Nuttersley would be halfway to school. Most children would take no more than five minutes to walk the short distance from the Nuttersleys' front door to the gates of Wormwold Primary School, but not Roy. He would prolong the walk for as long as possible by dragging his feet and observing the birds in the tall maples.

This coming weekend he would go to the timber yard for some more scraps of plywood to build yet more bird feeders. Sometimes the nice man in the brown overalls would cut the pieces to Roy's own specifications. As Roy shuffled through the green wrought iron gates of the school his heart began to sink. This was nothing new of course. He'd always feel like this when entering school. The headmaster, Mr Tonk had once said in school assembly that he wanted his school to be one big happy family. But Roy wasn't at all familiar with the concept of a happy family. His certainly wasn't. And neither was Wormwold Primary School a place he'd associate with happiness of any description.

The school building itself was a drab, grey affair with little in the way of charm or character, and wherever you set foot it had that distinct smell of boiled cabbage.

As the school bell clanged its dreary clang, Roy formed an orderly queue with the rest of his classmates. In truth though, none of them were mates at all.

Roy's class line shuffled into school like a row of ants and at precisely the same time Stanley Nuttersley arrived at his shirt factory. It had once been a church but now you could tell it was a shirt factory because it had a big red and yellow sign over the door that read 'Nuttersley's Shirts.' In smaller letters underneath were the words, 'Perfect Shirts for the Perfect Gentleman.'

Stanley Nuttersley brushed a blob of marmalade off his tie and pulled his heavy body out of his little car. Outside the factory was a group of very old ladies. They all had white hair. Some had walking sticks and one had a walking frame. These were the ladies who made the shirts in Stanley Nuttersley's factory.

"Good morning ladies," said Stanley in a jolly voice while he fumbled for his large bunch of keys to open the front door. He was really proud of his little workforce of old ladies. They may have been ancient, but they were highly skilled workers who knew how to stitch cuffs and collars and lapels and buttons - all the separate parts that go to make up a shirt. Besides, they were reliable and hard working too.

But more than anything else, he liked them because they were cheap to employ. Very cheap indeed. Having such small amounts to pay out in wages meant, of course, that Stanley Nuttersley could make more money selling shirts and this would often bring a broad smile to his chubby face.

Today was a special day. Today Cynthia, the lady with the walking frame, was going to turn eighty. So Stanley Nuttersley was organizing a surprise birthday party. He had already ordered the cake from the bakery. But unlike other novelty birthday cakes, this one wasn't going to be in the shape of a teddy bear, football pitch or steam train. It was going to be in the shape of a pink shirt with a nice big label saying 'Happy Birthday Cynthia' in green and yellow icing.

He had also asked the girl behind the counter to make sure that there was plenty of cream and strawberry jam sandwiched between the two layers of sponge cake. The very thought of washing down his afternoon tea with something a little more substantial than the usual chocolate biscuit or fig roll was now making him lick his lips. What could be nicer than a lovely big slice of yummy birthday cake, he thought to himself, as he opened the factory door and switched on the lights.

Roy, on the other hand, had nothing very nice to look forward to today. His morning was going to start with geography - YUK, followed by double maths - DOUBLE YUK. And before he'd had the chance to even set foot in the school he'd already received a nasty kick in the shin from Harry Hodges.

Harry Hodges was the biggest boy in Roy's class. He was also the meanest and most unpleasant specimen you could ever wish to set eyes upon. He lived on the big council estate near the school and his dad was in prison for doing something called 'GBH'. Roy wasn't too sure what this meant but it all sounded too horrible for words. And as a result, no one ever argued with Harry. Not even the teachers.

"Hurry up boys. To your seats and turn to page 24 of your textbooks. Today we are going to look at the very fertile area of Cambridgeshire known as the fenlands." Miss Hoxtead had such a dull, flat voice that she had the ability to make what already seemed like a very dull and flat subject fifty times duller and flatter than it already was. And judging from the photographs in Roy's textbook, the fenlands looked pretty damn flat and dull as it was.

The voice of Miss Hoxtead may have been irritating but at least it didn't cause Roy any physical pain. The same could not be said for Harry Hodges. After all, having established himself as the official school bully, Harry Hodges had to have someone he could bully on a fairly regular basis. And as luck would have it, that someone had turned out to be none other than poor Roy. So it was with a great deal of fear that Roy now turned his mind to his lunch break, since it was usually during this period that Harry and his cronies would set upon him.

Sometimes it would just take the form of nasty

threats, but on bad days Roy would receive what Harry called 'the full treatment'. This might involve the sprinkling of lots of pepper over Roy's school dinner, which he would then have to eat or, as Harry would put it, "suffer an even worse fate." There was, of course, a host of other treatments Harry might dish out at any given time. The thoroughly unpleasant punch in the tummy, kick in the shins or Chinese burn to the wrist, for instance.

After one particularly bad week, Roy had gone home, locked himself in his bedroom and composed a long letter to an organization called Amnesty International. He'd seen an advertisement in the morning newspaper and having read most of the text, had come to realize that this organization was able to help people who had been 'victims of torture.' He wasn't entirely sure what a 'victim of torture' actually was and why the sad looking man in the photograph was one of them, but he was quite sure that he, Roy Nuttersley, more than qualified.

The letter now sat crumpled up, lonely and unread at the bottom of Roy's sock drawer. It had taken a full two hours to compose.

Dear Amnesia International

My name is Roy Nuttersley and I couldn't help noticing your excellent advertizment in my dad's newspaper this morning.

I think you would be very interested to know that I am also suffering from torture. But unlike the unfortunate man in your advert, I am only 11 years old. So I think you would agree that I am a very young victim indeed. Anyway the person who is doing all the torturing stuff is a horrible boy called Harry Hodges. But I should menshion here that Harry's dad is a professional criminal who at this moment is in prison. So I would perfectly understand if you preferred not to take any acshion.

How ever, if you are feeling very brave and would like to take up my cawse and help me, you can contact me at the address at the top of this letter.

I wait for your reply with great antisipasion.

Yours sinserely

Roy Nuttersley

P.S. I am happy to be photographed free of charge for any future adverts.

Roy was quite pleased with the general thrust of his letter but couldn't help feeling that an organization that had the word 'international' in its title wasn't one that would very readily give its time to a victim suffering in the relatively comfortable surroundings of a primary school in the United Kingdom, rather than deepest

Africa or Eastern Europe. And for this reason the letter had found its way into the sock drawer and had remained there ever since.

THREE

The Birds

Birds are remarkable creatures. They have incredibly sharp eyesight that allows them to focus on small, wriggling worms from a very great height. They possess a fantastic sense of smell that can home in on the smallest crumbs of bread. And even though they aren't blessed with ears, their hearing is so good they can detect blades of grass being disturbed by the nimblest of cats. It was little wonder then that Roy's brightly painted bird boxes and feeders were beginning to attract the attention of all manner of birds.

The blackbirds sung Roy's praises to the sparrows, and the sparrows spread the word to the smaller birds. Before long, the excited chatter was to spread from treetop to treetop, from street to street, and eventually it would stretch beyond the clusters of little grey houses and reach the rolling green hills beyond.

As a result, the number of birds flocking to the little

garden at number 44 Orchard Drive was increasing day by day.

This afternoon, while the Nuttersleys were out of the house, the birds descended from the grey sky in huge numbers like tiny iron filings being drawn by a powerful magnet. But this was no ordinary gathering.

Countless birds and their precious nests of offspring were already appreciating Roy's handiwork and generosity. And now that the winter months were drawing closer, this remarkable haven would soon save so many of them the very hard task of scavenging for morsels of food for their cold and hungry families. All indeed was looking rosy.

But it was the perceptive blackbirds who, having used their beady eyes and sensitive hearing to the full, had noticed the unhappiness of the little boy. They had spotted his sad little face and his down-turned little lips that never broke into a smile. They had observed the shuffling feet and the downcast eyes each morning. But more than anything, they had picked up the noises from the Nuttersley household. While blackbirds would not admit to being experts on the subject of human behaviour, it was obvious to them that the high pitched shrieks from Mrs Nuttersley and the loud, booming bursts from Mr Nuttersley each morning, were not sounds that would suggest human happiness. And it was for these rather worrying reasons that the blackbirds had called the meeting.

By all accounts, it was a remarkable sight. The four

trees at Orchard Drive were now home to countless feathered specimens of all shapes and sizes. And for once, none of them had ventured to peck at the tasty contents of Roy's bird feeders. Instead they sat twittering and gossiping in anticipation of the arrival of the blackbirds. And arrive they did, all forty of them, to take their place on the upper branches of the mighty oak.

Within seconds of their arrival the commotion settled down and a hush descended upon all four trees. To the human ear, the pronouncements from the one single blackbird high up in the oak tree would have sounded like exquisite birdsong of great beauty. But to the birds themselves there was little beauty in what they were about to hear.

The remarkable song lasted for three whole minutes and when translated into human language sounded something like this:

"Dear and beloved family and friends...

"Firstly, I must thank you all for coming here today to hear me out. What I have to say is important, and I speak, of course, on behalf of all the blackbirds present...

"While we all remain grateful to the little boy - whose name I believe is Roy - for such acts of generosity, it has not escaped our attention that there seems to be a great deal of human unhappiness in this household. And this is something that should concern us all. For unhappiness, as we all know, is like a terrible disease that can take hold and affect one's behaviour in a very negative way...

"In short, my dear friends, if we allow this remarkably kind hearted little boy to become so very unhappy, there is every chance that his acts of immense kindness may be scaled down. Worse still, they may dry up altogether."

At this point, the silence of the birds was broken by agitated chirpings from the branches of all four trees. And it took an immense effort on the part of the blackbirds to restore order. However, this was eventually achieved following an impressive flapping of wings by all forty blackbirds. With the silence finally restored, the song from the top of the old oak tree continued.

"I know this is not what you wanted to hear, particularly now as the winter months close in on us. But the sooner we all recognize this situation, the better our chances of doing something about it...

"Our first course of action, therefore, must be to find out what is making this little boy so unhappy. Once we have established this, we will be in a position to reconvene and work out a plan of action...

"So I call upon the smaller members among us, the blue tits, the robins, the chaffinches and the house martins, to follow the movements of our little boy named Roy. I appeal to you to put your sharp eyes and agility to good use by observing all those he comes into contact with. We need to piece together a detailed picture of his typical day. Every morsel of information that you can bring back could prove vital in protecting the future of this haven...

"In seven days I suggest we all get together again. But with winter approaching, let us stretch the current seed supplies for as long as possible by feeding as little as we can from this special garden."

The song had come to its conclusion with a little trill. There was a pause. Then the blackbirds took their leave of the big tree. The other birds followed with an enormous flurry of beating wings and in an instant the mass of feathery bodies had dispersed into the grey, cloudless sky from where they had come.

The blackbird who had addressed them all had the furthest to fly to return to his family's nest. He swooped gracefully over rooftops, railway lines, roads and little patches of green playing areas and headed for the centre of town. On his way he glided momentarily over a parade of shops.

What he didn't know, of course, was that the corner building of this modest terrace was the shirt factory where Roy's dad worked. Although at the present moment, Stanley Nuttersley wasn't working at all. In fact, none of the people at Nuttersley Shirts were. Instead, they were seated around a large table; a table that was usually covered by various parts of disembodied shirts. This afternoon, however, a large flowery tablecloth with matching china teacups and plates had transformed the table. And at the centre, in pride of place, sat the magnificent birthday cake itself.

"My dear ladies. What can I say? As you all know, today is a very special day. It is Cynthia's birthday. She has been an inspiration to us all. Not only is she celebrating a very full and wonderful life, but today marks the thirtieth year that Cynthia has been with us at Nuttersley's Shirts." Stanley Nuttersley's eyes focused on the large cake and his stomach rumbled. "Yet during this time", he continued, "she has remained a loyal, reliable and priceless member of staff. In all these years, I can honestly say that I have never heard a bad word pass her lips. Cynthia, my dear, it is with very great pleasure that I present you with this card and small token of appreciation." Stanley Nuttersley twisted his large frame and recovered a large brown envelope from his seat. Then he stooped to pluck an impressive bunch of flowers from the floor beneath the table.

The tears in Cynthia's eyes welled up behind her thick glasses and rolled down her sunken cheeks. It was the first time she had cried in public for many years. The last time she could remember doing so was when her little Mickey was born all those years ago. She could still remember that little red face, pointed head and big blue eyes. He was such a beautiful little thing that she supposed he'd have made anyone want to cry. But now she wasn't so sure why it was that her vision was going all watery. Perhaps it was simply because she didn't like being reminded that she was old, and had left her best years behind her. When she was a schoolgirl she had been a lively young thing. She'd been captain of the school hockey team and had even been known to play football with the boys in her street - which in those days was almost unheard of.

Now her close friends were consoling her. Doreen handed her a pink tissue to blow her nose and Pat had her arm around her. Ronald, the driver had raised his glass and was smiling from ear to ear.

Stanley Nuttersley stooped awkwardly and planted two delicate kisses on either of Cynthia's cheeks. Then, though he knew he shouldn't, he leaned over the table and stretched his arm in the direction of the plate of sugary doughnuts. They had been freshly baked no more than fifteen minutes earlier and were still warm when he'd fetched them from the bakery. The trouble was he couldn't quite reach them. It was rather unfortunate that he couldn't because at the very same time, Cynthia had decided that she was going to give a little speech. Having taken firm hold of her walking frame, she thrust it purposefully to the floor to prove to herself that she still had strength in both her arms.

The sharp pain in Stanley Nuttersley's right big toe was excruciating. All thoughts of the sweet warm dough had now evaporated, along with his sense of balance. And like a large, motionless statue that had been suddenly struck by a double-decker bus, he now felt himself sway and then fall.

The crash was spectacular. Crockery jumped from the tablecloth, and biscuits, doughnuts and little triangular sandwiches managed to fling themselves in every conceivable direction. One jam tart somehow got catapulted so high in the air that it got wedged into a dusty air vent just below the ceiling. Stanley Nuttersley himself had fallen on the weakest point of the table with such force that he'd actually broken it in two. Despite this, the table legs remained intact and upright, so that the table now took the form of a large 'v' shape. And all the items that hadn't been propelled elsewhere had slid down the two steep sides of the tabletop and found themselves either lying next to or on top of Stanley Nuttersley, with the exception of the birthday cake.

The magnificent birthday cake that had been so lovingly laboured over by little Lizzie, the trainee at the bakery, had been transformed in an instant into a less than magnificent giant splodge. Most of this was now adhering to Stanley Nuttersley's ample bottom, and he could almost feel the cream and sticky strawberry jam oozing through his trousers.

To some extent, the accident, though shocking, came as a relief to Cynthia. After all, she had no idea what she was going to say in her little speech. She would be the first to admit that she wasn't very good with words anyhow. Now, of course, no one knew quite what to say. The owner of Nuttersley Shirts, the man whose name appeared on all the shirt labels, the very same man who paid their wages, was lying in front of everyone in a most undignified fashion in a puddle of cream and jam. What was there to say?

Stanley Nuttersley hated being the butt of any joke. But there was something he hated even more, and that was embarrassing silences in a room full of people. He hated them so much that he always felt compelled to talk about absolutely anything at dinner parties to fill these embarrassing gaps. He'd been known to talk about earthworms, garden manure, flying saucers, even pig farming - about which he knew nothing. And now, to his credit, he looked up at his bewildered staff and he chuckled. And the chuckle turned into a laugh. And the laugh became so infectious that it wasn't long before the entire room reverberated to the sound of laughter.

FOUR

A Bird's Eye View

Harry Hodges, the school bully, very rarely laughed. But then he had very little to laugh about.

The grim block of flats where he lived had been built in the late 1950s and was a particularly unpleasant place to be brought up. The public entrances and stairwells were often littered with rubbish, and no one ever used the lift because it always smelt of wee. And come the summer, all the mums would hang their washing over the sides of the dull brick balconies. In some ways this was a good thing as it would at least cheer the place up a bit; particularly during the hottest days when really bright clothes would drape the dull building in a brilliant patchwork of vibrant hues.

Many of the families living on the estate just had single mums and no dads. Those that did have dads often had dads who were out of work. And many of the kids would wander around in gangs at night with nothing better to do than slash car tyres, daub graffiti and steal cars.

Harry's gang just consisted of himself and two other boys. Brian Sampson and Colin Harmsworth were both relatively small and scrawny boys who lived on the same council estate. Together they got their kicks out of being thoroughly nasty to the other kids at school. In recent weeks they had derived a great deal of pleasure from picking on one boy in particular. Harry had singled him out as 'a sad little loner who was just askin' for trouble.' Roy, of course, was a natural target. He was quiet, not very big, and didn't seem to have any friends to speak of.

Now that school lunch was over and all traces of scmolina pudding and custard had been scraped from bowls, the children spilled out into the playground. Roy feared the worst.

The school playground was a fairly sparse area of greyness. A couple of old sycamore trees that had been saplings many years before the school had been built somehow managed to survive to this day, and now towered over the nondescript landscape. For the past week or so the branches of the trees had provided hundreds of small birds with the ideal place from which to observe and chat avidly about Roy. The blue tits, robins and chaffinches had all agreed that what they had seen was not at all encouraging. From the windows of the dining room they had witnessed the nasty treatments meted out to poor Roy. They had seen the punches, the kicks, the Chinese burns, and they had seen the genuine terror in the little boy's eyes. Today, however, they would see a great deal more that would trouble them.

As usual, the mass of little human figures in the grey playground engaged in activities of one sort or another. Many of these seemed to include balls of varying size and involved running around quite frantically. But one little figure would always separate himself from the mass and sit himself on a bench below the trees.

This afternoon Roy had brought his 'Book of British Birds' to look at during break. But he couldn't bring himself to read the words properly because deep down he knew that Harry and that gruesome twosome - as he now called them - would almost certainly have something in store for him.

The birds knew this too because, from their high vantage point up in the trees, they could already see what Roy could not.

Harry Hodges and his scruffy assistants had cunningly managed to slip out of the school gate and work their way around to the back of the school, and were now climbing up the playground wall like three agile monkeys. Harry always used to boast to his two loyal mates that he had three uncles in the SAS. "This exercise," he had told them, "would be somefink they'd be able to do standin' on their heads." Once all three had managed to scramble to the top of the not so high wall, they could enjoy a perfect view of Roy as he sat with his back to them.

"Right. Don't forget what I told yer", whispered Harry. "The element of surprise is what counts. If your enemy ain't expecting you to pay a visit, then he ain't gonna stand no chance, right?" Colin and Brian nodded enthusiastically to their leader.

From the sycamore trees, the little birds watched in horror as the three boys descended stealthily from the top of the wall and crept up on Roy. To the birds it was like watching one of their friends being stalked by three cats. The difference though, was that unlike any of their feathered friends, Roy seemed totally unaware of the danger he was in. Then again, even if he had been, his chances of escape looked pretty slim, as he didn't possess wings. In a desperate bid to draw Roy's attention to the situation, the birds began to shout as loudly as they could.

The twittering of the small birds caused Roy to look up at the trees above him. But as he did so, he received an almighty shock, because instead of seeing the trees' branches against a crisp blue sky, all he could see was the grimacing face of Harry Hodges bearing down on him.

What took place next was not at all pleasant. Harry got his arm round Roy's neck and the two accomplices got hold of his legs. Then they proceeded to dangle poor Roy upside down and shake him so hard that everything fell from his blazer pockets: conkers, loose change, pens and his treasured plastic binoculars. Harry scooped up the lot and stuffed them into his own pocket. Then they swung Roy by his hands and feet and threw him into an unhealthy looking bush.

"I fink Nuttersley here has been taught a good lesson don't you lads? But he needs to know that if he starts blabbing about this to anyone, then I'm afraid I will have to tell my dad. And if that happens his life won't be worf livin'. Do you get my drift Nuttersley?"

Harry had certainly caught Roy unawares and as a result he was in no fit state to give any kind of answer. Not that Harry was expecting one. All that occupied his mind at the moment was the dull pain in his right side where he had fallen, and the fact that his blue binoculars were no longer in his pocket. He was still in a state of shock as he pulled himself from the bush and retrieved his 'Book of British Birds' which was lying open nearby at the section on 'how to construct your own bird box' with a dirty great footprint across it.

The little birds had seen enough. They had gained a clear picture of Roy's tormentors and were now keener than ever to relay this information to the blackbirds.

FIVE

Food for Thought

Half a mile north from Orchard Drive lies Primrose Park - a pretty green space with its walled rose garden, boating lake and perfect billiard table bowling greens.

Over a hundred years ago it had been home to the Ingleby family who had acquired a small fortune by making brightly coloured buttons to adorn the petticoats and waistcoats of ladies and noblemen. However, when Mr Ingleby senior had died, the button business and large estate was inherited by Oliver Ingleby, the family's only son. Sadly, Oliver was a very lazy young man and had little interest in the family business, which he duly closed down and sold off. Over the next couple of years, he managed to single-handedly squander the entire family fortune by gambling it all away. As a result, the large house eventually fell into disrepair. And when Oliver died an early death in an unfortunate boating accident on the

River Thames, his younger sister inherited the dilapidated house and estate and was kind enough, as she was already rather wealthy, to pass it to the borough council as a gift to the people. So in 1925, it was opened to the public.

Today the house no longer stands but Primrose Park is well cared for and is home to countless grey squirrels, scores of mallard ducks and several families of Canada geese. And it was the Canada geese with whom the blackbirds now desperately needed to cooperate. After all, the distressing news of Roy's ordeal had meant that drastic action needed to be taken. And it needed to be taken very swiftly.

The forty blackbirds circled above the murky boating lake and swooped down to the moist grass beside the water. Yards away, two particularly fat geese sat contentedly gazing at the water. It was rare for them to exchange words with smaller birds, apart, of course, from the ducks who invariably needed to be asked in no uncertain terms to get out of their way on the water. On the whole, the geese were, as you'd expect, fairly antisocial creatures. So to receive a visit from so many blackbirds was a most peculiar happening. So peculiar, in fact, that the slightly larger of the two geese now choked on his rather late breakfast: a nice juicy worm.

"Do excuse us for this unannounced visit."

The blackbird's song had begun. But unlike the

previous song, this one was to last for some considerable time and involve more than one speaker (or perhaps we should say singer). Of course, the blackbirds knew that this was always going to be a very difficult challenge for them. Geese are notoriously stubborn and arrogant birds, and what the blackbirds had in mind was clearly going to take more than mere persuasion. Blackbirds, however, are very clever and can be exceptionally charming when they want to be. Indeed, other birds would sometime joke about the blackbirds' ability to quite literally charm other birds from the trees, which was a term they had picked up from humans.

So, first of all, the blackbirds began by wishing the geese well on the imminent arrival of their little ones. Then they made an amusing reference concerning the patter of tiny webbed feet. Moving swiftly on, they appealed to the vanity of the geese by referring to them as the pillars of the community, complimenting them in glowing terms on bringing up such fine young specimens and upholding the very highest standards of behaviour and decorum. This done, it fell to the eldest and wisest member of the blackbird community to change the tone.

The elder blackbird who had already addressed the large meeting at Orchard Drive, explained - in a far less sing-song fashion - the concerns they all had about the coming winter. He announced that there could be little doubt that the climate was changing and that winters were getting colder and pointed out that this was not just something the blackbirds had picked up from humans. They explained that they had seen it for themselves by observing that more resident birds were now upping sticks and moving to warmer climes, while fewer foreign speakers were arriving. In truth, the blackbirds didn't know this to be a fact, but they did know that no one liked to hear news that could seriously affect their livelihood - geese especially. So a bleak picture was painted by the elder blackbird. And the geese slowly began to envisage poor food supplies, a lake with a frozen skin six whole inches thick, and the unthinkable prospect of flying hundreds if not thousands of miles to find food in less severe conditions.

At this point, the blackbirds started to realize that their address was having an impact, for not only had one of the geese forgone his breakfast, but breakfast itself had now managed to escape back into the earth. Moreover, there were no longer just two geese listening intently, there were no fewer than a dozen. And a few more were now waddling most inelegantly towards the small audience to see what all the fuss was about.

The elder blackbird paused while the new arrivals took their place. The silence was also necessary as it allowed the geese to ponder on the seriousness of the blackbirds' words. If all this were true, would they be up to flying large distances? It was a difficult question for them to answer. They had lived here in Primrose Park all their lives and had never seen the need to fly huge distances. The very thought of emulating their ancestors and distant cousins who flew from the Arctic now made them feel very uneasy.

Sensing the tense atmosphere, the elder blackbird now chose to offer words of comfort. He outlined a very possible solution to this ominous development. He described the garden at number 44 Orchard Drive, the remarkable quantity of birdseed and the generosity of the little boy called Roy. Then he made it very clear that the seed supply, if regularly stocked up, would certainly see the bird community through the winter months. Flying half a mile would surely be better than heading for a foreign land many hundreds of miles away.

The geese couldn't have agreed more and nodded their heads on their long necks in appreciation.

But then, just when things were looking up for the geese, came yet more worrying news. The blackbird described in excruciating detail the terrible ordeal of their potential saviour - Roy Nuttersley. The kicks, the punches and the terrible shaking of Roy upside down were not only harmful to the little boy; they might seriously harm the bird community too. For, if Roy were allowed to become so unhappy and miserable, he might not continue feeding them. And it was for this very reason that the blackbirds had come to speak to the geese today.

"You see my dear friends," continued the blackbird,

"we have thought long and hard about this awful situation and come to the firm conclusion that the three unsavoury boys who are making Roy Nuttersley's life a misery will have to be dealt with. Indeed, if we do not succeed in stopping their terrible behaviour, we all stand to suffer the very grave consequences. And this, my friends, is where you come in. As we blackbirds see it, you have a unique opportunity to achieve great things. Oh yes, very great things indeed. My dear, dear friends, you could go down in history as the heroes of Primrose Park.

"I needn't tell you how utterly splendid, spectacular, even fearsome you birds can look when flying in 'V' formation. Particularly when flying low. The sound of your wings beating in unison and your terrifyingly loud honk are beyond compare. But you know, you possess one potent weapon that birds of our meagre size just cannot match. I refer, of course, to our bodily functions. Now, when we blackbirds feel the call of nature, the blemish we cause on the ground or upon a parked car is just that - a blemish, of no consequence. Half the time humans do not even trouble themselves to wipe the small splatters from the bonnets of their vehicles. But you, my dear friends, if I may be so bold, are the crème de la crème of flying bombers. Flying low over washing lines, you strike fear into the hearts of the humans down below. Of that there can be little doubt."

The geese were clearly feeling rather flattered by all this. They had never really given much thought to their own physical capabilities, but now that they did, they could understand why the smaller birds might be in awe of them. As for the rather delicate subject of bodily functions, they certainly knew how much humans hated it when their possessions received a good splattering from the heavens.

"So essentially, what we would dearly like you to carry out is a daring, daylight bombing raid on our three prime targets. We know from the detailed information we have been passed by the blue tits that the three culprits usually roam around together and can usually be spotted in the school playground at one o'clock, human time.

"But before carrying out this special mission, you will, of course, need to undertake target practice and spend some time perfecting your formation flying. Needless to say, the tricky bit will be choosing your moment of attack and limiting it to these three boys. Precision bombing is what is called for here. So I would urge you to start preparing for your big chance as soon as possible. Time is of the essence."

The geese, of whom there were now a dozen, sat motionless. It was a lot for them to take in. They weren't the most intelligent of birds but even they could see that the task in hand was vitally important, not only for themselves but the entire bird community.

SIX

Mr Tonk's Pride and Joy

Mr Tonk had been headmaster of Wormwold School for twenty-two years. It was an awfully long time for anyone to be in one job. But for Mr Eric Tonk it was especially long. You see, he didn't really like children. He found them a nuisance. And as a single man without children of his own, he couldn't quite see the point in having them. Children were hard work. As a rule, they were noisy, badly behaved, rude and generally quite messy. No, overall he was quite glad he didn't have any in his house. Having them run riot at school was more than enough, thank you very much. So when he'd return home each day to his immaculate, detached home with its privet hedge and neatly trimmed front lawn, it was like entering his own little version of heaven. The peace and tranquillity would descend as soon as he'd set foot through the door and his worries and anxieties brought on by that wretched school would simply evaporate like condensation on a windowpane.

Though he didn't warm to children particularly, Mr Tonk was nevertheless a very affectionate man when it came to Siamese cats, of which he possessed two, and was very taken with classical chamber music - especially string quartets. His other great passion in life was Arabella. This, you may be forgiven for thinking, was not his lady friend, though he would often refer to her as 'old girl.' Arabella was, in fact, a rather old but beautifully maintained motorcar that he had inherited from his late father. Built in 1952, Arabella was a majestic, black Bentley complete with an imposing radiator, two gleaming headlamps and graceful running boards.

So precious was Arabella to Mr Tonk that he very rarely got behind the steering wheel these days for fear of doing the car any harm. Instead, the car would be kept in the garage and would only come out on special occasions.

Today was such a day, since Mr Tonk was going to visit his Aunt Edith. As his father's only sister, Aunt Edith had virtually been a second mother to him as a child. And now that both his parents had sadly passed away, she was the nearest thing he had to a real mother. In fact, he still had warm and vivid memories of happy summer holidays spent building sandcastles on the beach with his aunt in Dorset, and fishing for crabs with her in the rock pools on the Norfolk coast; something his mother never actually did. So it was with a great deal of happiness in his heart that Mr Tonk now opened up his garage and climbed into the driving seat of his pride and joy.

It was a lovely sunny morning, though certainly cold. The sun hung low in the autumn sky and bathed the landscape in a crisp, golden light.

Mr Tonk turned the ignition key in the polished walnut dashboard and the large, solid engine behind the bonnet sprung to life with a deep, resonant purr. It was a wonderful sound that had never changed in all these years. And every time he turned that little silver key and heard that familiar sound, all those childhood memories would come flooding back to him. The trip with his dad to London zoo where the elephant stole his ice cream, and the picnic at Hampton Court where he'd got lost in the maze, and had to be rescued by the head gardener. It was funny how such little things could trigger so many wonderfully warm and happy feelings from the past, thought Mr Tonk, as he wiped away a tear. He eased the gear lever forward and gently rolled forward out of the garage.

Like her nephew, Aunt Edith had never married and was also rather fond of cats. She had lived at Pear Tree Cottage for as long as Mr Tonk could remember. It was a quaint little house with simple, whitewashed walls that came to life in summer with purple clematis and fragrant, pink honeysuckle. Set in the village of Little Babbington, it would take Mr Tonk no longer than an hour and a half to reach at a steady pace in the slow lane.

As the rows of smart, detached houses gave way to a patchwork of green and yellow fields, Mr Tonk sank into the comfortable leather seat and gave some thought to the day ahead. He couldn't have chosen a better day for a picnic, and he was hoping that his choice of location would meet with his aunt's approval. Had he remembered to include the thermos flask of lemon tea? Yes, he was fairly sure he had placed it in the boot between the hamper and fold-up chairs. What about the homemade raspberry jam – Aunt Edith's favourite? Yes, he was positive he'd put it in the hamper. He could relax. Everything had been taken care of.

Being a Sunday morning, the traffic on the road wasn't very heavy, so Mr Tonk found himself cruising along at a higher speed than he would normally be comfortable at. But then, this was easily done when behind the wheel of Arabella. She may have been over fifty years old, but once the engine was turning over, she'd roll along so smoothly that it could be difficult to tell quite how fast she was going - unless you kept looking at the speedometer, and this wasn't an especially accurate instrument these days.

While Mr Tonk cruised along the country lanes, immersed in his own childhood memories, Miss Edith Tonk was feeding her two babies. Clarence and Clarissa were two half-Burmese cats with elongated, pointed snouts, slender bodies and unusually long legs.

"There you are my dears." These were familiar words to Clarence and Clarissa. And each time they were uttered by their adoring owner, the cats knew immediately that some delectable treats would be appearing in each of their china bowls. Today they would not be at all disappointed. Both bowls were now brimming with succulent pieces of smoked salmon and Dublin Bay prawns. It was the least Edith Tonk could do. She was leaving her poor darlings to fend for themselves for the whole day, after all, and for this she had to admit that she did feel terribly guilty.

As a woman in her late seventies, Edith Tonk was a remarkable individual. She managed to go to her yoga class twice a week and still played the odd round of golf at her golf club. "Youth," as she always used to say, "wasn't an age, it was a state of mind."

Of course, she always looked forward to seeing her nephew and being driven by him in that wonderful car that made her feel like a member of the Royal Family. But she had no idea where he was going to take her today. Last time he had taken her for one of his little spins, they had ended up in Brighton and had enjoyed lunch in an elegant hotel overlooking the promenade. She had always had a soft spot for her nephew. He'd always been so generous and such good company, even as a little boy in khaki short trousers.

While Clarence and Clarissa licked their lips in contentment, the sleek black roof of the Bentley made itself visible above the top of the neatly clipped privet hedge at the front of the cottage. Mr Tonk turned off the engine and got out.

He pushed open the green garden gate and smiled to himself as it squeaked in its usual way. No amount of oil had ever stopped that gate from squeaking: it was almost as if it had a personality and will of its very own. On reaching the front door and placing his finger on the doorbell, something quite unexpected and actually rather terrible happened. You see, instead of Mr Tonk's ears being greeted by the gentle ding-dong of Aunt Edith's doorbell, they experienced something altogether louder and nastier. It could only be described as an enormous honking sound. And it caused Mr Tonk to virtually jump out of his skin. He spun around in shock and caught a glimpse of the most incredible sight. Scores of large geese, flying very low and in a 'V' formation, were heading straight for him and as they did so a torrent of black globules came raining down from the sky. Then came another sound, a sound that could have passed for a dull and prolonged drum-roll being played not on a drum, but on a large sheet of metal. Mr Tonk cowered in the doorway, his hands shielding his eyes in fear. But mercifully, the large birds had flown over his head.

"Ah Eric, how lovely to see you my dear. Bang on time as usual. Do come in." Aunt Edith had opened the front door. But as she spoke these words, she couldn't help noticing that her nephew was not quite himself. "Are you feeling well, my dear? You look as if you've seen a ghost."

Eric Tonk straightened his tie. But before he could

reply to his aunt's question, Edith's eyes fell on the roof of the black Bentley. Only from where she was standing the roof didn't look very black at all. "My word, Eric, have you had that lovely motor car of yours painted white?"

Mr Tonk turned and peered at the roof of the car that protruded above Aunt Edith's neatly clipped hedge. To his horror, it did look white - very white indeed.

The geese were, of course, feeling jolly pleased with themselves. It had taken a few days to get used to flying in formation, but their efforts had certainly paid off. The sight of that black car being bombarded with reasonable accuracy, and the look of utter fear and astonishment on the face of its owner was most reassuring.

Now, as the cold air blew directly into their beady eyes, the geese, all forty of them, nosed upwards towards the wispy clouds and headed for home.

Mr Tonk, on the other hand, wasn't going anywhere at all. Instead he looked open mouthed at the foul mess that had been made on his beloved motorcar. Never for a moment did he think that Arabella would be harmed by anything other than another car - let alone a flock of low flying geese. But at least the damage was not permanent. And as he stood scratching his chin while mopping the cold sweat from his brow, Aunt Edith appeared from the corner of his eye wielding something long and green in her hand.

"This should do the trick my dear." And with these words there came an impressive squirting of water.

Aunt Edith had always been an incredibly practical person, so it wasn't surprising that she should now be dousing Mr Tonk's car with her garden hose, which was usually employed for her prize dahlias.

SEVEN

A Plan is Hatched

The news of the successful daylight training operations of the Canada geese spread in no time at all. Naturally, the blackbirds in particular were extremely pleased to hear this. From the very start they had had grave doubts over the ability of the geese to carry out this mission; and they had good reason to think this. For a start, persuading these stubborn birds to do anything at all was always going to be an uphill struggle for the blackbirds. And even if their persuasive powers were to prevail, there was no guarantee that the geese would be up to the task in hand. They had never really flown in formation for any great distance, and neither had their parents. They were lazy, good for nothing birds who had become accustomed to the easy life - lolling around Primrose Park without a care in the world. They probably wouldn't be capable of flying very far even if they wanted to.

So you can imagine how surprised and delighted the

blackbirds were then when word got back to them that the first practice run had been a huge, unmitigated success, and that the target in question - a rather unusual and out-of-date black car - had received no fewer than thirty direct hits.

When all was said and done, however, no one could have been more surprised by these remarkable achievements than the geese themselves. How exhilarating it had felt to stretch those wings and fly in formation. And how easy and natural it had seemed.

It wasn't long before news of their endeavours would reach the wider community of geese, and in time their numbers would swell to an impressive eighty adults and twenty-five youngsters. In short, enough birds to form a fearsome low flying squadron: one that would undoubtedly strike fear into the hearts of all those human dots below, careless enough to fall into its shadow.

Not that any of this was going to affect the way in which three scruffy boys were to behave over the next few days. They had no knowledge of the plan that had now been set in motion. And even if they had, they would have laughed themselves silly at the preposterous idea.

Their behaviour, though very bad indeed and not at all excusable, was also understandable. You see, you have to understand that little boys unfortunate enough to be brought into this world by parents who really had no wish or desire to be parents at all, were themselves victims of the most terrible cruelty. After all, when parents do not have the decency to show any interest or the remotest sign of love and affection towards their children, we can hardly expect these poor children to behave normally. Particularly when the family home is a thoroughly run-down place where gangs and petty criminals lurk at night. To put it another way, you need to ask yourself this simple question: how would you feel if your parents had no feelings for you; didn't care in the least where you were and what you were doing; and took no interest in your education? It is more than likely that you, too, would feel angry. And so it was with poor Harry Hodges and his two mates. Unfortunately, in their case, this anger was not channelled into productive activities like sport or art or even studying, but was expressed instead by doing damage and harm to everything and everyone around them. Strangely though, these acts of anger - whether bullying Roy Nuttersley in the playground or slashing car tyres in the multi storey car park – didn't make Harry and his mates feel any better in the least. It just made them want to carry out more acts of recklessness. It was like some terrible addiction for which there seemed to be no obvious cure.

Their very latest acts of anger and frustration had been felt by no fewer than fifteen smartly dressed men and three equally well dressed ladies. All eighteen of these unfortunate individuals happened to drive very smart, shiny cars. Unfortunately for them, though, these cars were no longer looking quite so smart. For a start, all eighteen of these machines now had flat tyres, but perhaps more disturbingly, they also displayed across their sizeable bonnets two crudely air sprayed black letters: 'H H.' It had been the largest, most daring operation Harry and his loyal chums had ever carried out. But despite the impressive scale of this latest act of vandalism, Harry was feeling totally unsatisfied. As far as he was concerned, there could be nothing more satisfying than the simple and brutal act of bullying someone rather than something.

"What's the point of slashing rubber and messing up paintwork? I mean, cars don't feel a thing do they?" Brian Sampson and Colin Harmsworth shrugged their shoulders. It wasn't the kind of question they were used to hearing. Harry kicked a crushed Coke can hard against the wall.

The two other boys stared at their scuffed trainers.

"Loads of kids do stuff like this anyway. Shouldn't we be a bit more creative? You know, get ourselves noticed, hit the headlines maybe?" As he uttered these words, Harry kicked the crushed can as if he were taking a penalty for Arsenal in an imaginary FA Cup Final, this time sending it over the side of the balcony outside Colin's front door. All three boys peered over the side as it clattered to the ground below.

"What d'ya mean?" asked Colin.

"I dunno," said Harry.

Brian, who hadn't said a word until now, suddenly

spoke. "I know," he said. The two others turned their gaze to Brian who sat on the floor chewing gum. "We could kidnap Roy," he said as if it was the most natural thing in the world to suggest.

There was silence.

Those four simple words had hit Harry like an enormous upper-cut right between the eyes. Why hadn't he thought of it himself? It was a mad idea, of course, but everyone knew that mad ideas could sometimes be the most brilliant. Just like that bloke who'd had that mad idea of inventing a bouncing bomb during the war.

If they were able to kidnap Roy they'd not only grab loads of attention, they'd be able to demand money too from those stupid looking parents of his.

"You must be off your rocker mate," chipped in Colin. Harry gave him a look of disapproval and Colin shut up.

"No. It's not a bad idea. Just think. We'd make headlines in the papers." Brian smiled to himself; it wasn't often that Harry would acknowledge any of his ideas as being anything other than hare-brained.

"But Harry. We could go to prison if we got caught," protested Colin.

"Don't worry mate. We're too young for that. And anyway, if we did get caught – and there ain't no reason why we should - we can always say that it was all just a silly joke that went a bit wrong."

Harry's answer didn't sound terribly convincing to

Colin, but this serious and obvious flaw in the plan didn't seem to matter anymore. The gang of three now had an exciting and truly daring mission to prepare themselves for. Their lives had suddenly found a new purpose.

What they didn't know, of course, was that their every movement was being carefully monitored, not by the plethora of security cameras that we have all become accustomed to in our high streets and public places, but by the small beady eyes of blue tits, house martins and robins. Indeed, unlike the large, cumbersome devices we humans rely on to record poor quality images of those who are up to no good, the blackbirds could bank on a far more sophisticated collection of highly mobile and ultra sensitive spies. In this respect, the blue tits were invaluable as they were in fact the only birds that could understand the strange vocal sounds that humans produced.

So when, several days later, the three boys were to spend much time in the school playground sitting on the very same bench that Roy usually occupied with his book of 'Book of British Birds,' the blue tits had already positioned themselves on the lower branches of the sycamore trees. And it was from these lower branches that the detailed plans of Roy's imminent kidnap were now shared with those nimble little acrobats sporting powder blue and pale yellow bellies.

The plan was simple enough. Colin would tell Roy that if he wanted his blue binoculars back he would have to pay Harry £5 in a secret place, out of view behind the caretaker's hut at one o'clock. Once Roy had been lured to the meeting place, the three boys, out of sight, would put him in the caretaker's wheelbarrow and cover him with a tarpaulin. Then they would push their victim across the school playground and through a hole in the far fence where they could get into the adjoining allotments. Once here they could quite easily gain access to one of the several garden sheds that were not currently in use, and padlock Roy in. The whole scheme had been thought up by Harry. Little else had occupied his mind over the past couple of days. And now that he divulged his plan in its full glory to his two partners in crime, he could tell by the looks on their faces that he had won them over.

Colin, however, did have one question. "But what happens if someone asks us what we're doing?" he asked.

Harry had thought of this. "We just tell 'em that we're helping out old Mr Partridge by wheeling some of his tools up to his allotment." Mr Partridge who taught history was the school's oldest and most doddery teacher. Yet despite his bad back and arthritis in his right knee, Mr Partridge spent many hours each week on his allotment next to the school. And last year his giant pumpkin won first prize.

It was, of course, a brilliant answer. For once in their lives they'd look as if they were carrying out an act of kindness. So no one in their right mind would want to stop them doing that, surely. Both Colin and Brian acknowledged this devilishly cunning answer and seemed completely satisfied that the plan was a sound one. All that remained for them now was to decide on a day. Colin suggested the following Monday. "Monday," as he put it, "was the most boring day of the week and needed livening up." The other two had a certain sympathy with this view. But on reflection, Harry decided that Monday may have been the worst day of the week, but it was also the only day of the week that the dinner ladies ever served up lamb chops or beef burgers with chips. And seeing that they were going to have to forgo lunch to kidnap Roy, Monday was looking distinctly less attractive.

"Tell you what," said Brian. "Why don't we do it on Wednesday?" Harry and Colin looked at each other quizzically. Then they looked at Brian.

"Why Wednesday?" asked Harry.

"Well, that's when we get served that 'orrible stinky yellow fish with mushy Brussels sprouts," replied Brian while pinching his nose and scowling as if he could almost taste the offending dish.

He had a point. If they were going to miss lunch, this was one lunch they certainly weren't going to mind missing for one minute. So on the basis that yellow haddock and Brussels sprouts were universally loathed by all three of them, the fateful day of Roy's kidnap was agreed upon. The following Wednesday it was.

The blue tits, of course, couldn't believe their good

fortune. Not only had the three scruffy boys discussed their vile plan in the open air, they had done so most conveniently in the shade of the sycamore. What's more, they had revealed everything the birds could possibly have wished to know in one short session.

So the prospect of having to lip-read from a distant window or maybe having to fly inside the school building to find out more about the boys' plan was no longer a concern for them.

The house martins, whose grasp of the human language was very sketchy to say the least, sat impatiently, waiting for the blue tits' translation. When it finally came, they couldn't contain their excitement for a moment longer. They hopped from branch to branch and chirped with joy.

As far as the three boys were concerned, everything was going according to plan. The problem was, the plan itself was no longer just theirs.

EIGHT

Mrs Nuttersley's Dastardly Decision

Mrs Angela Nuttersley was a creature of habit. She had a very fixed routine that she followed religiously. Breakfast was always followed by a series of domestic chores including washing, hoovering, ironing, dusting, polishing and lastly but by no means least, cooking. She was so fastidious about all these activities that she wouldn't entertain for one moment the idea of employing a cleaner to carry out any of these vitally important tasks, for she knew deep down that no matter how scrupulous and ruthlessly efficient an employed cleaner might be, she could never live up to her own very high standards.

In fact, she had had countless nightmares on this very subject and had woken up at night on several occasions in a cold sweat, having experienced very vivid visions of discovering a couple of hairs protruding from a plug hole or a thin film of dust revealing itself below the legs of the carriage clock on the mantelpiece.

And it was now, as she vigorously polished the kitchen windows with a soft yellow cloth, that she focused on the colourful collection of bird feeders hanging from the trees outside. She was sure there were more of them hanging today than she had noticed before. They were pretty enough, she thought. But just as she was thinking these thoughts there came a distant ding from the large tumble dryer underneath the sink. This immediately drew her attention to the fact that the newly washed bed sheets would now be dry. However, the thought of nice clean bed sheets and the view before her very nose set large alarm bells ringing in the back of her skull. The notion of hanging out the washing on warmer days with so many bird feeders attracting birds from near and far suddenly sent a shiver down her spine. It wasn't right. She couldn't possibly allow her precious laundry to delicately flutter on pleasant days in such close proximity to so many birds. Not that she had anything against birds, of course. But it would clearly be a foolish thing to encourage so many of these feathered creatures to come so close to freshly laundered fabrics. There was no knowing what terrible mess they might leave on them as they flew overhead. So it was with these thoughts rattling around in her head that she marched out into the garden wielding a large pair of scissors in one hand and a stepladder in the other.

It was unfortunate but, there really could be no other solution. She opened the stepladder and seated it firmly into the grass below the smallest tree and began to climb. Snip, snip, snip, snip.

Umpteen weeks of Roy's creativity was now being undone in no time at all, as one brightly coloured bird feeder after the next fell to the ground, spilling birdseed here, there and everywhere.

High up in the old oak tree five blackbirds observed Mrs Nuttersley's actions with utter disbelief. All their well-laid plans were now being completely undone too. For all this time, they had feared that Roy's tormentors would pose the biggest threat to this special garden. Never in their wildest dreams had they imagined that the little Nuttersley woman with her irritatingly high-pitched voice could have been the real threat all along.

As the little coloured feeders continued to fall from the overhanging branches, the blackbirds sat motionless as if glued to the spot. Within minutes, Mrs Nuttersley had efficiently stripped the trees of their decorative wooden houses and deposited them all in a large cardboard box with the words 'Tebworth Tinned Peaches' emblazoned across its side. Now she dragged the large box across the bumpy lawn and opened the rickety garden shed. Next both she and the box disappeared inside. This was followed by the sounds of much thumping and shuffling from within, and finally Mrs Nuttersley re-emerged with a large broom, the handle of which was taller than its owner, and an equally long handled rake. With these two implements she set about clearing the mess left behind on the grass by neatly piling the offending birdseed into three small mounds. This done, she replaced the tools back inside the shed and then made her way back into the house.

The blackbirds who were still sitting motionless hadn't uttered a single tweet. For once, all five of them were completely lost for words. And then, as one of them prepared to break the silence, Mrs Nuttersley reappeared from the house, this time clutching a large grey upright implement of some sort with a very long tail of wire, which trailed behind and disappeared into the house. She carried this very peculiar looking item onto the lawn and then pushed it gently, for it clearly had wheels, in the direction of the trees. Once she had positioned it over one of the mounds of birdseed, she flicked a switch and the ugly looking device sprang to life with an even uglier and raucous voice of its own that gave the birds such a shock that they all immediately leapt from the oak tree for the refuge of a neighbouring maple. From here they could see that this terrible machine clearly had a ravenous appetite, as it now seemed to gobble up all the birdseed with ruthless speed and efficiency. Above the ghastly noise, the blackbirds could even hear the sound of the birdseed rattling around its cavernous tummy.

It was all too much for the blackbirds. They had seen enough.

While most birds would have no doubt accepted the

fate of their little haven in Orchard Drive, the blackbirds could not. It was not in their nature to simply roll over and accept these things. It was a trait that had held them in good stead over the years, and it was precisely why other birds, no matter how large or small, would always look to the blackbirds for answers. And it was answers that they desperately needed to come up with now.

It was clearly going to be a tall order. So much so that when, a couple of hours later, the blue tits managed to finally track down a large group of elder blackbirds at Primrose Park, their sudden and very excited arrival didn't receive the kind of enthusiastic welcome they would normally have expected. Indeed, the mood seemed most sober.

"My dear friends, I am afraid your sudden arrival has come at a very grave time for us all."

This lone voice belonged to the very eldest of the blackbirds, and he spoke slowly and carefully with a deep resonant chirp.

NINE

Digging up the Past

Brian Sampson was usually a sound sleeper. He had to be with all the noise and commotion that would go on either inside the flat or outside on the estate. It never really stopped. If it wasn't his two older brothers arguing with their mum it would be shady characters doing shady deals out on the street while slamming car doors – which was their way of announcing to those indoors to stay exactly where they were if they didn't want trouble. But Brian's difficulty in getting to sleep on this particular evening had little if anything to do with the noises going on around him. The reason was simply this: tomorrow would be Wednesday - the day that all three of them were going to kidnap Roy, demand some kind of ransom and get their faces pasted all over the newspapers, and possibly even the television news.

And to think all this was his doing. If he hadn't suggested kidnapping Roy in the first place, they'd probably be planning something really boring, like painting graffiti onto the garage doors of posh houses in Buttercup Drive, or nicking the badges off smart cars.

But, more importantly, for once in his life, Brian was feeling valued by someone. Admittedly, that someone was only Harry Hodges. But that didn't matter. It was still something special. Well, no one usually valued a single word he'd say - not that he ever said very much. His parents certainly hadn't ever taken him seriously. All they ever did was tell him to do chores or 'stay out of their hair'. And as for his teachers, they were no better. All they ever did was tell him to stop doing stuff. Stuff like 'being a disruptive influence in the classroom' or 'chewing gum' or 'daydreaming.'

Brian closed his eyes. But it was no good. There was no way he was going to get to sleep.

Half a mile away from Brian Sampson's bedroom that sat high up on the sixth floor of the council block, was another small boy who couldn't get to sleep. His bedroom though wasn't as high up since it was only on the upper floor of a 1930s suburban house. And this particular household wasn't at all noisy and neither was the neighbourhood.

Through the boy's window, you could just discern the intricate network of black branches thrown out by the mighty oak against a full moon. Roy never liked to close his curtains at night because he felt closer to nature, and that was something that always comforted him. And tonight of all nights, he certainly needed comforting.

It had been a perfectly acceptable day at school. He hadn't been so much as scowled at by his tormentors. In fact, Colin Harmsworth had actually sidled up to him in the corridor that morning and said in a conspiratorial whisper that Harry wanted to give him his blue binoculars back, and suggested that Roy meet Harry behind the caretaker's hut the following day at one o'clock. Then as an aside, he had told Roy to take a few quid with him. "Five should do it. Just to keep Harry sweet," were the words he had used.

Then Miss Allen had marked his essay with an A* and had read its contents to the whole class. Roy had enjoyed writing the piece. It was all about the old man who used to do the gardening for his parents. His name was Albert and he was the oldest man Roy had ever known. Poor old Albert could never quite stand straight due to some terrible bone condition and found walking difficult without the support of his bicycle, which looked as old and weather-beaten as he did. But the extraordinary thing was that he was as strong as an ox, despite his condition and mature years. And he could do the garden as well as any man - if not better. Sometimes, when Roy took him tea and a jam sandwich that his mum had prepared, Albert would lean on his garden fork and regale Roy with real and vivid stories about the war.

During the war, Albert hadn't been fit enough to be a soldier, so instead he had helped the fire brigade and ambulance crews rescue people from houses that had been bombed and set ablaze by German airplanes. His proper title was Air Raid Precaution Warden and he must have been incredibly brave because he never thought twice about going inside burning buildings during an air raid to rescue survivors. And it was one of these stories that had now worked its way onto paper and become Roy's very own.

The story had been firmly planted in Roy's mind. It certainly wasn't a story you could have made up. It took place sometime during the height of the London Blitz when the German bombers were bombing the city relentlessly night after night. Albert had returned home from his day job at the bank where he was a clerk and had been called out after a particularly heavy bombing raid in the Whitechapel area, close to where he lived.

On arriving at the scene of devastation with his mates, Albert made his way to a large, blackened shell of a building that was engulfed in flames and smoke. But before strapping on his metal helmet and diving fearlessly into the burning wreck, he had been drawn by an innocent looking china doll in a tatty red dress lying on the ground among the rubble. Its face was smeared with dirt and grime, yet its bright blue, innocent eyes gazed, wide-eyed and oblivious to their surroundings. For some unaccountable reason Albert had stood transfixed by the object and had then started frantically removing rubble from where he was standing.

The entire street had been littered with the debris

and dust that had once formed solid brick walls, wooden window frames and front doors.

While his colleagues ran ahead, yelling at each other, and the thick plumes of smoke were made even thicker by the huge cascades of water pumped by the firemen, Albert focused on the mound of rubble at his feet.

With his bare hands, he pulled at boulder after boulder. Within minutes, his frantic efforts were beginning to take their toll on his poor hands, which were now becoming caked in blood and dust. But this did not deter him and his efforts, if anything, became even more frenzied. And then, as if by some miracle, Albert's bloodstained hands encountered something soft to the touch - fabric.

Now he worked even more vigorously to reveal a large swathe of red velvet and then a small leg: the leg of a child. Before he knew it, he had quite literally unearthed a small girl, perhaps four or five years of age. Like the china doll, her dress was red and her delicate face was also smeared with filth. But unlike the china doll, this larger version didn't have her eyes wide open. Albert felt the little girl's blackened wrist and prayed. The world around him stood still. The commotion and turmoil faded away as all Albert's concentration now centred on that little limp wrist. And then he sensed it. There was no denying it. It may have been faint and distant, but his grubby fingers, though sore and aching with pain, had detected that constant and unmistakable pulse. The girl was alive. And Albert had screamed like he had never screamed before.

Saving the little girl was one story that Albert loved to tell. And he told it so well, with so many intricate details, that it didn't matter how many times you had heard it before. Like an old film you knew the ending to, it would never fail to capture your imagination and draw you in. And now that Albert had sadly died, there was no one left in the world to tell his story. So Roy had sat down in his bedroom and had summoned all his energies in an attempt to pour into the piece as much emotion and detail as Albert would have done while leaning on his fork.

His spelling may have left a great deal to be desired, but his written piece had clearly worked. As Miss Allen uttered the final words of Roy's story, she removed her delicate designer spectacles and wiped her right eye with the sleeve of her cardigan. The class sat speechless and then, one by one, the children began to clap instinctively. It was the first time anyone had ever been clapped in the classroom by the other children. And it was the first time Roy had ever received an A*.

So, all in all, Tuesday had been a remarkably good day. Until, that is, he returned home from school.

The sight of those bare trees, stripped of their carefully crafted bird feeders came as a sharp blow to Roy and the thought of fewer birds in the garden made his heart sink.

His mother's callous actions and complete lack of understanding didn't help matters. Nor, of course, did

Roy's obvious and rarely expressed anger. So it wasn't long before that piercing voice of Angela Nuttersley's would sing out, that the rafters would shake, and that poor Roy would be sent to his room without supper. And it was here that Roy now turned on his pillow, which was still damp from his tears.

TEN

Operation Blitzkrieg

The past 24 hours had been a testing time for the blackbirds. There was no doubt that the current crisis had put enormous pressure on these intelligent birds to provide an intelligent solution.

The solution they had finally agreed upon could not have been more ingenious and devious. These cunning birds had quite rightly assumed that Roy would try his hardest to persuade his mother to replace the bird feeders on the trees. And they had also correctly assumed that he would not get his own way. With these calculated guesses established, the blackbirds, after the liveliest of debates, concluded that Mrs Nuttersley needed a distraction of enormous proportions. A distraction so momentous that she would forget about the bird feeders altogether.

And so it was that the blackbirds went in search of those flamboyant, extrovert and often argumentative characters: the magpies.

Meanwhile, at ground level, back at Orchard Drive, Roy was undertaking a search of his own. He could have sworn that he had left eight pound coins in his small Spiderman wallet with the Velcro flaps and enclosed pockets. But try as he might, he just couldn't find it anywhere. He opened his three drawers and rummaged through his school clothes, sweatshirts and underwear, but it was nowhere to be seen. And now his mother's piercing shriek came from the bottom of the stairwell. "Hurry up you foolish child, and get yourself down here this instant. You will be late for that infernal school of yours!" It was no good. He would have to forget about the blue binoculars today. So he ambled down the stairs, head bent and dejected, and picked up his school bag that was lying half open in the hallway. As he did so, there came another piercing outburst from the kitchen, this time directed at his father. "You complete, blithering idiot – look what you've gone and done to the tea towel." Before his father had a chance to start his counter-offensive, Roy had closed the front door firmly behind him and was halfway down the garden path.

The day, though not especially sunny, was brightened when Roy arrived at the school gates. Of all the people Roy could have possibly imagined waiting here to greet him with a broad smile, Harry Hodges would certainly have been the last. But here he was with his tie at half-mast and his hair gelled back. "Just thought I'd congratulate you on that essay of yours," he said and stuck out his grubby hand to shake Roy's. "I hope you're going to be able to make our little meeting at one o'clock."

Roy pulled his hand away and stuttered. "Oh. Yes. Well... I would. Only..." Harry gave Roy a suspicious look.

"What's up Nuttersley? Cat got your tongue?" Roy looked at his shoes.

"Well you see, I don't have any money to pay you." Harry laughed.

"That's alright mate. Don't you worry. I fink I can let you off this once." And with these words Harry slapped Roy on the back and ran off in the direction of the allotments, turning momentarily and shouting back, "See you at one then."

Roy couldn't believe it. Harry was actually being nice to him. It didn't make any sense. One moment he was being shaken upside down and thrown into a bush, and the next he was being treated like an old mate who was the salt of the earth. Could a simple piece of writing really have that effect on someone? If it could, thought Roy, surely there would be far fewer wars going on in the world. But then, didn't someone once write, 'the pen is mightier than the sword'? Perhaps they had. And perhaps whoever it was that had, had a point. After all, there were loads of wars fought over religion, and all religion amounted to was a lot of written words. So maybe he should write an emotional piece to his mother pleading with her to let him resurrect his bird feeders in the garden.

With these thoughts in his head, and with his school bag still half open, Roy filed into the school.

Overhead, a couple of large distinguished looking birds perched on the sycamore: their magnificent purple black plumage set off by their dazzling white breasts. The magpies had never ventured into the school playground before. Well, it wasn't really their scene. But this was a necessary reconnaissance exercise. They had already had a good look through the windows of the garden shed at Orchard Drive and seen for themselves the brightly coloured bird feeders piled into a very large cardboard box. Now they wanted to catch a glimpse of Roy Nuttersley himself.

He was a fairly small, unremarkable child, just like the blackbirds had described him. It wasn't that the magpies distrusted the blackbirds, it was just that they were pernickety birds. It was in their nature to satisfy themselves that every detail they had received had been accurate. In other words, every 'i' had to be dotted and every 't' crossed. Had they been human beings they'd most likely have been accountants, or civil servants, or those people who sat behind the counter at the post office.

Everything did indeed seem to be in order. And it did look as if the large quantity of bird boxes and feeders that had been crammed into that cardboard box would certainly have provided an enormous quantity of food. The blackbirds had not exaggerated.

So now, as the final child disappeared into the drab

looking school building, the two magpies contemplated the two tasks they had been set.

Essentially, the first of these would not have been at all difficult had it been summer. The blackbirds' request for a nice silk tie could have been quite easily satisfied during the warmer months by plucking one from a suburban washing line. But finding one at this time of year was a completely different matter.

As for the gold ring, this was always going to be a hugely challenging task, even for the talented magpies.

Quite what the blackbirds had in mind with these two items was impossible for the magpies to fathom. All they did know was that the blackbirds were exceptionally smart, and were admired by one and all for their intellect. And unlike so many of the other birds, they had principles and could certainly be trusted to keep their word.

If the magpies were able to keep their part of the bargain, then they were sure that the blackbirds would keep theirs. And on this basis, the challenge that now presented itself was one they were going to have to face up to.

As the two birds headed skyward, Roy caught a fleeting glimpse of the two magpies as they worked their way across the large windowpane of the classroom. Little did he know that the actions of these two distant specks would ultimately have an enormous impact on his life.

While Roy sat in his maths lesson, idly composing in

his head a possible letter to his mother, Harry Hodges was making final preparations for their big plan. He had managed to saw through the feeble metal bar that held the padlock to the door of the caretaker's hut with a small hacksaw. Once inside, he was relieved to find the large green wheelbarrow, plenty of strong gardening string and a selection of tarpaulins neatly rolled up in the corner. Everything was set. All he had to do now was discreetly secure the door with tape.

The morning passed quickly enough. Maths was followed by a relatively lively history lesson about the Vikings, which was followed by religious education. This, though a little dull, did at least give Roy an opportunity to finish composing the letter to his mother.

By the time his next lesson - English with Miss Allen - had begun, the distinctive and rather unpleasant smell of that yellow haddock from the nearby kitchens was already making its presence felt. This, however, hadn't even registered with Roy. In fact, all that really had registered with him was the fact that a small white rectangle now hung from the wall in a rather splendid gold frame at the front of the classroom.

It was his essay. Miss Allen had gone to the trouble of framing his essay – no one else's. And now she began to explain at some length why she had done so. Roy, it appeared, had set what Miss Allen called 'the benchmark' for essay writing. "Or put another way," she said, "the highest level so far achieved by any individual in the class." The idea was that everyone now had to try their hardest to set an even higher standard by writing an even better piece, she said. Though this, she thought, may prove rather difficult. And so it was that at the end of this lesson, Roy was in a very good mood. For a start, Harry Hodges had been nice to him that morning, Miss Allen had framed his essay, and now he could look forward to receiving from Harry his prized binoculars. But the thought of his binoculars now brought the whole episode of his mother's appalling act sharply into focus. There were no two ways about it. He was going to have to send the letter. And the sooner he did so, the better.

He strode confidently out of the classroom and headed straight for the caretaker's hut, and on arriving, was greeted by the three scruffy boys, all of whom smiled broadly like three Cheshire cats.

As Harry stepped forward, there came into view a quite extraordinary sight. He wished he had his binoculars there and then, because if he was correct, and he was pretty sure that he was, there in front of him and behind the heads of the three grinning boys, was the most impressive formation of Canada geese. He'd never seen anything like it. There must have been at least a hundred of them. It was awesome. But the very odd thing was that they now seemed to be getting lower and lower. And they were heading directly at them. Roy stood fixed to the spot.

"You alright mate? You've turned as white as a sheet." Harry and his accomplices now positioned themselves close to Roy so that they would be able to grab him quickly. But before Roy or anyone else had a chance to say another word, there came the most deafening sound from the vast squadron of geese that was now fast approaching its target.

The next few seconds were very unclear to the three would-be kidnappers. Roy had thrown himself with considerable force at the three boys standing in front of him, as if he were playing rugby for England. It was in fact the perfect tackle, as all four of them were now sent hurtling through the feeble looking door to the caretaker's hut, and landed with an almighty thud to the floor.

Roy didn't know quite why he had reacted as he had. It was what some people might have called a spontaneous reaction. He had simply sensed danger and acted accordingly.

It was lucky for all four that he had. For what happened next defies description.

While the four boys lay on the floor in the half light of the caretaker's hut, there followed a rapid, machine-gun like succession of thuds above their heads, and the hut seemed to shudder under some kind of barrage from above. The boys instinctively put their hands to their heads as if they were re-living Roy's vivid account of the London Blitz.

Then, as abruptly as the barrage had begun, it suddenly came to an end.

Slightly dazed, Harry was the first to disentangle

himself from the others, brush himself down and venture outside.

The first thing that struck him was an overwhelming and quite sickening smell that was so strong that he had to hold his hand over his mouth and nose. As he did so, his feet made a horrible squelching noise as he tried to lift them from the grass. This, he could now see, was due to the fact that he was standing in a large puddle of revolting slime. The awful mess not only covered much of the grass, but had also splattered over large areas of the caretaker's hut. In fact, it was still dripping in large gloopy globules from the roof and was making its slow descent down the windowpanes of the hut.

Harry felt physically sick. And as he surveyed the scene before him, there came from above the loud, though now distant, sound of honking. He looked to the sky and could see the enormous formation of Canada geese, black against the sun. And it was now that it dawned on him that the fate of the hut had been meant for him and his accomplices. Had it not been for the sharp reactions of Roy, the very boy they were about to kidnap, things might have turned out a thousand times worse. Even worse than that perhaps. Who knows what evil poisons and hideous diseases lurked in this foul slime? Had he been covered in this noxious gunk from head to toe, he might have ended up in an isolation ward of a hospital with some dreadful exotic disease. For all he knew, he might have needed loads of tubes stuck into him like those road accident victims he'd seen on TV hospital dramas. He might have even died.

In truth, these thoughts were having an even more unpleasant effect on Harry than the dreadful slime itself. Although he would never admit it to anyone, including himself, what he was actually feeling at the moment was the most awful feeling of guilt. It wasn't something he'd ever really experienced before. And it wasn't something he ever wanted to feel again.

By the time the three other boys had re-emerged from the ramshackle hut, Harry, like the geese, had taken flight. He needed to feel the cold air in his face, as if in some magical way it might cleanse the dark feelings he now harboured in his head and in the pit of his stomach. Besides, the last thing he could bring himself to do just now was look Roy in the eye.

ELEVEN

The Thieving Magpies

After a succession of grey, miserable days that were so typical for late autumn, today looked very promising indeed. The sun shone through the thin curtains of Mr Tonk's bedroom and had fragmented into small patches of bright dappled light that now spread themselves, for the time being at least, across large areas of Mr Tonk's bedroom wallpaper. But it hadn't been the sunlight that had stirred Eric Tonk from his slumbers this morning: it had been the two elegant creatures that Mr Tonk shared his immaculate home with.

Delius and Dvorak, those two self-centred animals with their silky pale coats and chocolate brown paws and snouts, had made their presence felt earlier than usual. And so it was that Mr Tonk now found himself in the kitchen donning his silk dressing gown and less than exotic paisley slippers.

Having prised open the can of 'Catykins' which

according to the label consisted of an 'exceptionally fine blend of chickens' and calves' livers for the discerning feline,' Mr Tonk delicately spooned the less than exceptional contents into the two separate bowls on the floor. And as he did so, the two animals pushed their noses greedily into their respective breakfasts. This first mechanical, though important task, complete, Eric Tonk was about to head off to the bathroom, but was stopped in his tracks by a small blinking orange light. "Oh. Hell's bells," he cursed to himself. He had completely forgotten about the washing machine that had finished its washing cycle the previous day and had obviously remained on all night. At least the sun was shining, he thought to himself as he now removed the damp items from the drum and placed them in a large plastic basket.

As Mr Tonk stooped over the blue washing basket, two magnificent magpies swooped down from the heavens and perched themselves comfortably on the branches of the old cherry tree that had been planted at the back of Mr Tonk's garden almost half a century ago by the previous owner. Their efforts over the past couple of days had proved both gruelling and fruitless. But then, it was hardly surprising. No bird in their right mind could have expected humans to hang out their washing at this time of year. Today though, was different. The crisp, golden light given off by a low hanging sun made everything look as warm as toast.

The two birds who were by now feeling quite tired

and distinctly peckish, had spotted the old cherry tree and lush, green lawn with its thin coat of morning dew from afar. It looked to them like a perfect place to take the weight off their little legs and have a scout around for juicy worms.

So it was something of a surprise when the garden door of the house suddenly opened and a figure of a man in his dressing gown stumbled out onto the patio clutching a large basket of washing. Any plans the birds had had to search for breakfast were instantly put on hold.

The man who was clearly rather tired took his time to hang up the washing, of which there seemed to be an enormous pile. Large, pale shirts and endless pairs of drab looking undergarments were meticulously pegged onto the washing airer. As the mountain of washing was slowly reduced to a small mound, the two birds sat motionless, gazing intently at each item as it was removed from the basket.

It seemed like forever. But just when the washing airer looked like it would not accommodate one more single item, there came from the basket two slivers of silky fabric: one pale lilac with emerald green spots, and the other deep burgundy with golden stripes that twinkled in the sunlight. The two magpies could not believe their luck as these two attractive ties hung temptingly like two oversized worms before their very eyes.

The man shuffled in his slippers back into the house

and closed the garden door with a click. The two magpies had, by chance, found their precious prize. But before they could attend to this, their appetites badly needed satisfying. It was time to look for worms.

It was some hours later that Mr Tonk was to finally notice the missing items from the washing line. It wasn't that he was a particularly perceptive person, because he wasn't. It was just that he was rather sentimental. You see, in themselves, those ties may not have seemed at all special. But to their owner they were very special indeed. The pale lilac one with emerald green spots had been given to him by none other than his father when he had taken the job at the school all those years ago. The other, though in remarkably good condition, was even older, and had been given to him by Aunt Edith on his 21st birthday. So in some small way these two thin slivers of fabric formed a significant part of Eric Tonk's life. That was how he saw it at any rate.

As he stood on the patio with the washing basket at his feet, he scratched his head in puzzlement. The two plastic pegs that had held the ties in place were now lying on the grass.

While Mr Tonk grappled with the mystery before him, two large magpies physically grappled with two long slivers of fabric in mid flight. Neither of the birds had ever attempted such a feat before. Flying with these long and slightly damp items trailing behind them was far more difficult than they could possibly have imagined. In fact, the weight and air resistance created by the two ties meant that each bird had to flap its wings twice as hard as usual to simply stay in the air. It was exhausting work, which required regular breaks. But their efforts were now beginning to pay off as the two ties slowly dried out in flight, and became considerably lighter to carry.

As the two birds now headed towards the large clump of trees outlining the perimeter of Primrose Park, the weather took a distinct turn for the worse, and the magpies now found themselves flying into a strong wind. And it was this sudden gust that had caused the pale lilac tie with its emerald green spots to free itself from the tired beak of its current owner. There was nothing the magpie could have done about it. The piece of silky fabric danced a curious dance in the pale blue sky, twisting this way and that. It was just as well that the two birds had managed to find two excellent specimens because the wind was now carrying the liberated tie on a journey of its own. A journey that would take it across large swathes of dull, grey suburban streets, railway embankments, a small cemetery with a lovingly tended rose garden and a couple of giant, garishly painted DIY warehouses constructed from corrugated metal.

Meanwhile, the magpies pressed on in the direction of Orchard Drive. The old oak tree was, of course, a useful landmark for the Nuttersleys' garden since it towered above the rooftops and other trees and stood out like a sore thumb. And it was here on one of its many solid outstretched arms that the two birds now perched with relief; their little hearts beating furiously.

The problem they now faced was how to plant the tie. The idea of flying into the house was clearly one that filled them with dread. Getting in through an open window was difficult enough, but getting out would pose the real challenge. Besides, they ran the almighty risk of encountering the human inhabitants, and that in itself was a life-threatening prospect that neither of the birds would have wished on their worst enemy. Then there was the memory of their dear cousin who not so long ago delved into the chimney stack at number 32 Orchard Drive and was never seen again. Naturally, this particular incident still haunted them.

Inside the house, all was calm and as quiet as a mouse. Mrs Nuttersley peered out of the garden window from Roy's bedroom while sipping her first cup of tea of the day and smiled to herself. There were noticeably fewer birds in the trees and shafts of sunlight were filtering through the branches of the overhanging trees and casting puddles of bright light on the small lawn.

At first, the birds hadn't noticed the innocuous looking object on the grass. But now, as they gained their breath back, they could identify in the shadows on the lawn a very familiar looking item. Rather than blue, however, this plastic basket was grey, and there could be little doubt that its contents were destined for the washing line.

It was enough to prompt the magpie with the tie still firmly held in its beak to act very swiftly indeed. For birds have an uncanny knack of sensing an opportunity when they see one —magpies especially. The timing of the bird's response could not have been better, for as luck would have it, just as Mrs Nuttersley had turned from the window to rinse her empty cup under a running tap, the bird had swooped down and deposited its catch on the top of the neatly piled mound of washing in the basket.

TWELVE

An Act of God

For the past couple of days, Harry Hodges had avoided his mates altogether and had not even set foot inside the school. He needed peace and solitude. But more than this, he needed time to collect his thoughts. He'd seen some fairly incredible things in his life, but the episode with those geese was something else. It seemed like some form of supernatural happening. Bizarre, spooky, unreal: these were words that sprung to mind. You'd normally only see things like that on the big screen while munching popcorn, he thought. It bore little resemblance to real life. But then, of course, he kept having to tell himself that it was.

Now, as he gazed out at the boating lake on Primrose Park and squinted at the couple of geese flapping their large wings on the water, he wondered whether these specimens before him had taken part in the bombardment. Then it occurred to him that perhaps

Roy could have been some kind of wizard and possessed special powers that allowed him to communicate with birds. For a few moments the idea seemed plausible. Until, that is, Harry reminded himself that Roy was also in the line of fire. So that theory was hardly likely. And anyway, nobody in their right mind ever believed stuff like that.

As he sat there on the park bench with its peeling green paint, he began to feel cold and instinctively shoved both his hands into his jacket pockets. It was then that he felt the distinctive object nestling among a couple of conkers and a key ring. He pulled out the blue plastic binoculars and looked at them with a distinct feeling of guilt.

Roy had saved him from a fate worse than death. And yet all Harry had ever done for Roy was inflict bruises and stolen his binoculars. The kidnap plan made him feel even worse. For once, Harry was actually finding it hard to like himself very much. Until now, being horrible to others hadn't really bothered him in the least. People were generally pretty unfriendly, unhelpful and arrogant. And those who did try to show that they cared, like a couple of left-wing, muesli eating teachers, just seemed to be going through the motions and were so namby-pamby and insincere that Harry would have gladly hit them in the mouth. There was of course a world of difference between saying something and actually doing something. Actions, as some bright spark once said, spoke louder than words. And it was clear to Harry now that the only person who had ever done anything genuinely decent for him was the very boy he'd been bullying. It was ironic, almost funny. Though it didn't make Harry want to laugh. Far from it.

He bent forward to pick up a small flat pebble to see if he could skim it across the lake towards the geese. But before his fingers could so much as reach the grey stone, Harry felt a most peculiar sensation around the back of his neck as if a large feather had just brushed him. Instinctively, he put his hand to the back of his neck, and as he did so he could now see that a tie had draped itself perfectly around his neck. A pale lilac tie with green spots. Where on earth had it come from? He looked around him expecting to spot Colin or Brian, but instead saw nobody at all. The place was totally deserted, apart from an old lady walking her equally old dog on the other side of the lake.

Harry pulled the tie off his neck. It had a rich silky feel to it as it ran through his fingers. He turned it over and studied the label. 'Il Prescelto' seemed to be the trademark. It sounded foreign. And in smaller type were the words 'Pure silk. Made in Italy.' It was a smart tie - there could be no denying that. But how had it arrived out of thin air and why had it selected him, of all people, Harry Hodges? For a moment, a cold shiver ran down his spine and a sea of goose pimples spread themselves across his entire body. Could there have been a connection between the geese and the tie? Was this all part of some larger message being sent to him from a superior life force: aliens perhaps? Then his mind turned to the murky world of religion and those individuals who had always looked so ridiculous to him: the Muslim women dressed in black from head to foot with only a tiny pillar box slit for the eyes; the orthodox Jews with their funny broad rimmed hats, long beards and tassels; the Sikhs with their curious turbans; and those biggest fruit cakes of all, the Hare Krishna brigade in their daft orange robes, whose incessantly stupid chanting and drumming could always be heard a mile off. Perhaps they all weren't so stupid after all. Perhaps they knew something Harry didn't. Perhaps there was such a thing as a God. And perhaps this very God was talking directly to Harry, talking to him directly from the sky above.

Harry screwed up his eyes and looked up into that vast ocean suspended above his head. Large billowing cloud formations filled his entire field of vision. They moved ever so slowly as if stuck in a celestial traffic jam that was going nowhere very fast.

At first there seemed very little to look at. But the more intently he looked, the clearer the image became. He could see the eyebrows now, the high cheekbones and the strangely bulbous nose. And setting off these distinctive facial features was an unmistakable and majestic beard. Could he be in the presence of the Lord Almighty himself?

Harry closed his eyes, as if deep in prayer. But in truth his mind had gone blank. When he opened his eyes he couldn't reconstruct the bearded face from the drifting clouds. It had disappeared quite literally into thin air. For some unaccountable reason he was feeling in a better state of mind. It wasn't that he felt any less guilty about the way he had behaved towards Roy. The guilt was clearly still there. But now it dawned on him that Mr Tonk had had a point when in school assembly last week he had droned on about the importance of faith. "God," he had said, "has a tendency to move in mysterious ways." Too right, thought Harry. It was probably the first time he'd found himself agreeing with a single word that the headmaster had ever pronounced at morning assembly.

Harry took the tie and did something he hadn't done since his granny's funeral three years ago; he put it on. It actually looked pretty good, he thought, apart from the fact that he was only wearing a T-shirt and jeans. Then he took another look at the label. The words 'Il Prescelto' had a distinct Italian ring to them. He said the words to himself over and over again, feigning what he thought was an Italian accent. He wondered if the words had any meaning, or whether it was just a brand name like Tesco or Sainsburys. He would need to find out. But first of all, he would have to return the blue binoculars to Roy.

As Harry now sprung from the park bench with a new sense of purpose in his stride and looked down admiringly at his newly acquired tie, Mrs Nuttersley climbed the stairs of her 1930s semi detached home, clasping the fully laden washing basket.

She may have been perceptive when it came to matters of domestic hygiene and general cleanliness, but as far as her husband's wardrobe was concerned she had something of a blind spot. While a lurid pink shirt or glittery lame jacket may have struck her as odd for her husband's rather bland tastes, a wine red tie with a discreet gold stripe wouldn't have seemed at all out of character. In fact, the tie, which now lay on the top of the washing pile was so innocuous that she didn't even give it a second glance or a moment's thought. And so it was that at precisely 2.35pm Mr Tonk's beloved burgundy tie was transported to Stanley Nuttersley's wardrobe and now hung alongside eleven other ties, none of which were burgundy coloured or, for that matter, striped.

Stranger still was this: Mr Tonk's favourite tie - the pale lilac silk one with emerald green spots - now hung round the neck of a scruffy young man in a white T-shirt who was sitting in a slightly dingy cafe.

Harry had never been inside an internet café before. As he sat self-consciously with a cup of something the girl called 'cappuccino,' he peered at the screen. He usually only spent time in front of a computer to play violent 'shoot 'em up' games, and was sorely tempted to try his hand at the latest version of 'Armageddon 4' but restrained himself. It was just going to have to wait. He nervously found a suitable search engine and keyed in the words 'Italian Dictionary.' In an instant the screen filled with countless possible pages to choose from.

Harry just clicked on the first one which brought up a green and red website designed like the Italian flag. Carefully he typed in the characters: I...l... space P...r... e...s...c...e... l...t...o... Then he clicked the search button and in an instant the English translation appeared on the screen.

The sound of the ceramic mug smashing against the stone floor broke the silence and the girl behind the counter put down her 'News of the World' and went in search of the mop and bucket. "There's always one isn't there?" she muttered to herself. By the time she had got to the table with her cleaning items, Harry had gone, leaving behind him a brown puddle of cappuccino on the floor among pieces of the broken mug. The girl patiently cleared the mess and checked that nothing had spilled onto the keyboard. It looked perfectly dry to her, so that was lucky. Then she ran the mouse over the mat to check that it was working. And at this point, she couldn't help noticing the bold words on the green and red screen. They simply read: 'The chosen one.' She thought nothing of it and wiped away the last traces of coffee. This done, she tutted in an exaggerated fashion and addressed the other customers. "It takes all sorts don't it, eh?"

To say that Harry had received something of a shock would be putting it mildly. Until that moment, the notion that God might be talking to him by moving in 'mysterious ways' was no more than a vague possibility that he was toying with. Now, of course, there could be no question that this was the case, and that God had spoken to him directly via the internet. He was indeed 'the chosen one'. But chosen for what precisely, Harry wasn't at all sure. What he could be sure of though was this: his hands were shaking; his legs had gone all wobbly; he was sweating; and there was a large damp coffee patch on his trousers in a very embarrassing place.

THIRTEEN

The Uninvited Customer

Since the episode with the geese, Roy's life at school had become rather more pleasant. Harry Hodges, for a start, hadn't so much as smirked at him for some days now. Come to think of it, Roy hadn't even noticed him. And as for Brian and Colin, they seemed to be keeping their distance.

The bombardment of the gardening hut had certainly been a remarkable incident to have witnessed. Though the school caretaker probably wouldn't have seen it in quite the same way. Apparently, it took the poor man an entire afternoon to clean up the considerable mess, for which he had to employ an industrial jet spray and wear special protective clothing.

Roy had made several visits in his spare time to the local library to find out as much as he could about the habits of Canada geese on the computer. But his efforts trawled very little other than a letter posted on a community website in Vancouver, Canada that dealt with what the author called 'the terrible nuisance of these infernal birds.' It had been written by a retired gentleman whose garden lawn had been targeted by Canada geese on a regular basis. And as a result, he wanted the Canadian government to allow him to seek revenge on the birds with his twelve-bore rifle. From this Roy could only assume that while the incident concerning the gardening hut may have seemed highly unusual to most people, it would not have surprised the man with the ruined lawn one little bit. So on this basis, Roy put an end to his research, accepting that Canada geese can and do occasionally go on spectacular bombing raids.

Life may have become easier for him at school but as far as the Nuttersley household was concerned, he wished he could have said the same. The sad truth, of course, was that things had become significantly worse on the domestic front. For a start, there was a distinct lack of birdsong from the small garden each morning. It was a small detail perhaps, but such small and enchanting details count for a lot when you are a shy, ungainly eleven-year-old boy with a sensitive nature and very few friends in the world to speak of. Then there was his parents' relationship, which now seemed to be going from bad to worse. In fact, there was hardly any china left in the cupboard, since most of it, including a 60 piece dinner service that had been a wedding present, had now been thrown by Mrs

Nuttersley at her husband. This meant that breakfasts and suppers were now eaten from plastic picnic ware which, to be perfectly honest, had seen better days. Even the delivery of the small brown parcel with Roy's name on it the previous day had failed to fire him with much enthusiasm.

"Come on boy. It's not every day that you get sent a parcel with your name on it," his mother had yelled at him from the bottom of the stairs. Roy still hadn't forgiven his mother for her act of vandalism and had refused to speak to her - not that he ever said a great deal to her at the best of times.

Inside the parcel had been the pair of blue binoculars. Roy had forgotten all about them. But what had intrigued him more than the binoculars themselves was the accompanying note, which had been painstakingly written by someone who clearly wasn't used to writing.

Roy had read it carefully.

Dear Roy

I am returning these binokulers which I don't need no more.

Me and the others would also like to thank you big time for shuving us out the way of those horribel birds in the nick of time. I am sorry on behaf of me and the others for wot we did to you. I can see now that it was not very nice or at all nessessery. I do hope you axept this apolodgy. And I do hope we can be frends.

To prove that I mean wot I say I have pinned a fiver to this letter.

Yours most sinceerly, H Hodges

PS: You wont see very much of me for a while as I have some very serius bisness to do.

Roy still couldn't believe that Harry had actually said sorry. He didn't think the word was in his vocabulary. And as far as the crumpled five pound note was concerned, Roy was completely and utterly mystified.

Now, as he sat on his bed, he read the letter again, but it still didn't make any more sense. Why should Harry suddenly want to say sorry, be friends and pay him five pounds? Could this all be down to the simple fact that Roy had had the good sense to push Harry and his cronies out of the way of a flock of geese? Surely not. There had to be some other reason. And what had Harry meant when he'd said he wouldn't be at school because he had serious business to attend to? It all smelt very fishy. Very fishy indeed. Perhaps this was all part of some awful plan that Harry had devised to put Roy off guard. Still, the good thing was that Harry was clearly going to be off the scene for a while, so Roy didn't have to worry too much about all this - for the immediate future at least.

From down below he could hear his parents arguing

as usual over some insignificant domestic chore that hadn't been completed to Mrs Nuttersley's satisfaction. It was all too much for poor Roy, particularly on a Saturday. He took the five pound note from the envelope and shoved it deep into his trouser pocket. Then he ambled nimbly downstairs and let himself out of the front door.

He didn't have any plans to speak of. He just needed to get outside and away from that stifling atmosphere inside the house. As he reached the end of Orchard Drive a bus pulled up to the bus stop at the end of his road, and without a further thought Roy got on.

The bus was relatively full Roy thought, and then he remembered why. It was market day, so most of the people on board were after their fruit and veg or cheap socks. It wasn't exactly his idea of fun but the decision had been made for him by the bus on which he now sat.

It wasn't an especially large market but it never failed to attract hordes of people - chiefly old ladies with shopping bags on wheels who were on the lookout for bargains.

Roy weaved his way past the vegetable stands with their impressive displays sitting amid acres of green nylon grass and the hardware stands with their brightly coloured mops, brushes and brooms. The noise was incessant. "Get your luverly pand of mush." "Two for a pand. Two for a pand." "Come on darlins. Everythin' must go." Amid the noise and bustle, Roy had a look at the book and CD stall, which was being manned by a tall young West Indian man with impressive dreadlocks. As Roy became engrossed in a worn copy of 'The Bird Watcher's Companion,' there came a terrible commotion from another stall. A large balding man with a tight fitting T-shirt and a very red complexion was flapping his arms frantically and shouting abuse. This sudden outburst had the unusual effect of causing all the other market traders to become quiet as mice.

"Come back you thieving blighters. Come back. I'll have you, you thieving blighters! D'you hear me?" The man was extremely distressed, and had inadvertently attracted a throng of people to his stand who were obviously curious to see what all the fuss was about. Roy too had been drawn to the man's stand. Before he could reach it though, he noticed a beautiful magpie gracefully gliding above the heads of the shoppers. But it wasn't the iridescent streak of purple plumage that caught Roy's eye. It had been a gleaming golden sparkle. And it had come from the bird's beak.

By the time Roy had reached the stand, the man with the red complexion was sitting in a fold-up chair and was being consoled by two women police officers. Behind him was a long wall of padded red velvet on which countless pieces of golden jewellery seemed to be pinned.

"Fourteen carat gold. Eight carat diamond. Beautiful. And now it's gone."

As the man uttered these words, one of the policewomen copiously took notes. "Did you notice what he looked like?" she asked. There was a pause as the man wiped a tear from his eye.

"Him? What d'you mean 'him'? I couldn't tell if it was a him or a her. It was a flippin' bird wasn't it?"

FOURTEEN

The Nuttersleys Lock Antlers

The morning of Tuesday, 17th October will live in Roy's memory for a very long time to come. For this was the morning that Stanley Nuttersley rolled out of bed, opened his wardrobe and through bleary eyes, gathered his clothes for the day. It wasn't until he was fully dressed and was combing what little hair he possessed over his pink and shiny forehead, that he noticed the tie around his neck.

It was as if the man he was looking at in the mirror was someone else entirely. "What the dickens is this?" he boomed as his wife rolled over in bed.

"Oh do shut up you irritating lump of lard," she retorted in her usual less than charming manner.

For once, her words hit a nerve and instilled in her husband a rage that was far greater than Roy or the poor neighbours had ever known. This, of course, had little to do with the words Mrs Nuttersley had uttered and everything to do with the fact that Stanley Nuttersley was now wearing a strange man's tie around his neck. His thoughts raced as he tugged at the tie to remove this foreign item from his person. Who was his wife seeing behind his back? How long had it been going on for? And was this stranger being entertained in his very bed? These were questions he wanted answers to.

The problem, of course, was that the more Angela Nuttersley laughed at her husband's accusations and told him he needed the services of a psychiatrist, the more angry he became. And the more she denied any knowledge of another man in the house, the less he believed her.

"I suppose you expect me to believe that it appeared out of thin air," he bellowed.

As you will know, he wasn't far from the truth. But neither he nor his wife knew this. Indeed, at this point, his wife simply came to the swift conclusion that her husband had made this all up in order to divorce her. And she said as much.

The two of them were so convinced that the other was up to no good that the verbal exchange soon became ugly and physical, and before long they were both on the bed clobbering each other with pillow cases. While the screaming and yelling intensified, the air became thick with a mixture of goose and duck feathers.

With this awful commotion taking place next door to his own bedroom, Roy decided that it was time to leave for school earlier than usual and forgo breakfast. As he walked down the street, the sound of his parents fighting could still be heard - and as he looked back in the direction of the house, he could see a constant stream of little white feathers billowing out of the upper window of his parents' bedroom. It was a bizarre sight, and one that was causing several passers-by to stop in their tracks and have a good look.

By the time Roy had got to school, Stanley Nuttersley was wedged into his little car and was sweating profusely. He could barely contain his temper as a young pregnant woman pushing two toddlers in a double buggy took her time crossing the pedestrian crossing in front of him. "For heaven's sake do hurry up woman. I haven't got all day you know," he bellowed out of the side window.

At length he came to the factory but instead of pulling in and parking in his usual place, he went straight past it, even though the little old ladies were patiently waiting for him to open up.

He carried on for two blocks and then turned right at the lights, eventually drawing up at a small building with a dark glass window and a sombre looking fascia above the door that read 'Treadwell Fiddler and Partners.' He slammed his car door with more force than usual and barged through the front door of the building. Inside a blonde girl sat behind a desk painting her nails in a garish shade of pink nail varnish. "Can I help you?"

Stanley Nuttersley looked at the girl with a certain distaste. "No. I don't think you can. But your employer may be able to assist."

The girl stopped painting her nails. "I see you have a sense of humour. What's the name?" she asked.

"Nuttersley. Stanley Nuttersley," he replied. While the girl pressed a few buttons on her telephone, Stanley Nuttersley studied the cheap framed prints on the wall. They were poor reproductions of well-known paintings.

"I'm sorry Mr Nuttersley. Mr Fiddler is far too busy this morning to see you," announced the girl. "Can I make an appointment for another time later this week?"

"No you certainly cannot." As Stanley Nuttersley spoke these words he walked straight past the girl like an out-of-control bulldozer and pushed open the door to the side of the girl's desk.

Inside was a large man sitting at a large desk eating a large doughnut. "Mr Fiddler. It's good of you to see me at such short notice. The name is Nuttersley. Stanley Nuttersley. And the thing is, I need a divorce."

Stanley stuck out his hand, but the man behind the desk started to choke on his doughnut.

Back at Orchard Drive Angela Nuttersley threw herself into the household chores with even more energy than usual. It was her way of letting off steam. She couldn't believe the audacity and utter foolishness of her loathsome husband. How did he think that he could get away with accusing her of being unfaithful? Not that the idea wasn't appealing, of course. As far as she was concerned a divorce would suit her down to the ground. But there was no need to have invented some stupid story. It was childish. Though this, she thought, was probably being a little unfair to most children who undoubtedly had more sense than her husband.

She put on the kettle and made herself a cup of tea. She would need this to unwind from this morning's events, which had tested her nerves to breaking point. As she opened the garden door and let herself out, her mind turned to the possibility of her husband divorcing her. This, she thought to herself, would be a very positive turn of events. After all, she would be able to stay in the house with Roy and her husband would have to live elsewhere. She plonked herself down onto the plastic chair on the patio and placed her mug of hot tea on the plastic table.

Then her heart nearly missed a beat. Because there, sitting on the table no more than a couple of inches away from where she had placed her mug, sat an extraordinarily beautiful diamond ring.

It was obviously the property of another woman. So that conniving, two-faced, fat husband of hers was the one who had been seeing someone else behind her back all along. And that was why he was so keen to create a story - any story, no matter how absurd - just so that he could divorce her and start a new life with some other woman. It was all becoming terribly clear now. How careless this new girl must have been to have left this piece of evidence lying on the plastic table. But how fortunate for Angela Nuttersley that she had. Now she would show her husband. She'd do everything in her power to make life difficult. She'd refuse to divorce him. If he wanted a divorce he'd jolly well have to take her to court.

She grinned to herself as she thought these thoughts. Then she took hold of the diamond ring and held it up to the sky. As its many facets twinkled brilliantly, she could see that it was certainly a fine specimen. In fact, it was clearly a lot larger than her own engagement ring, which obviously annoyed her a great deal. Goodness knows how much money her revolting husband had spent on it. Perhaps he'd got down on his knees and proposed to this mystery woman. The idea made her shudder. With these very negative thoughts in her head she took the ring upstairs and then, without any further thought, dropped it in the lavatory bowl and promptly pulled the chain.

The household chores would now have to wait. Angela Nuttersley had far more urgent matters to attend to. She opened the top drawer of the antique dresser in the hallway and pulled out a fat telephone directory. She scanned the page that opened under the heading of 'solicitors' and her eye fell on various names: Bartholomew Marcus and Partners, too posh sounding she thought; Treadwell Fiddler, too dodgy. And then for no other reason than it sounded bland and safe, she picked up the telephone and dialled the number for a firm by the name of Noble, Barker, Price and Partners.

FIFTEEN

The Parting of the Ways

Harry Hodges had been missing now for four days. His mother who spent most her time shouting was only now registering his absence. If she wasn't shouting at Harry's two older brothers, who tended to either shout back or simply ignore their mother altogether, she'd be shouting at someone or something else, whether it was a neighbour, the people at the DHSS, or the television set. "Where's that bleedin' monkey of a brother of yours?" she bellowed at her elder sons, both of whom merely shrugged their shoulders. "He'd better show his face soon, otherwise his father's going to get to hear about it. And then he'd wish he'd never been born."

It wasn't one of the most logical statements Mrs Hodges could have made. Harry's father was, after all, behind bars and wasn't expected to come out for some considerable time. So even had news of Harry's disappearance reached the ears of his father, there would have been very little Eric Hodges could have done about it.

As it happens, Harry was in the process of writing to his mother. It was going to be much easier to say what he had to say on paper than finding the right words to deliver down the phone. Besides, it would deprive her of the opportunity to shout back at him.

He pulled up the chair to the simple wooden desk, scraping the stone floor in the process, and began to scribble away. Outside, the rain came down in sheets and dribbled in channels down the small, latticed window above him. It was a cold, damp place to have found refuge. But deep in his heart, Harry felt at peace with the world. If he was to talk seriously to God, this had to be the place from which to do so. There could be little question of that.

High above the old rafters was the old belfry, and above this sat the crumbling roof tiles originally made by the monks themselves, which were now covered in moss and lichen. And sitting on the very top of this pile of history sat one exceptionally tired blackbird.

It had been the most arduous of flights. The poor bird had had to follow a bus and a train. Thankfully, the bus hadn't been too difficult to keep pace with on account of the fairly regular stops. The train, though, had been another matter altogether. In fact, the blackbird had very nearly given up hope of ever catching Harry up. But blackbirds aren't birds to give up easily, and this particular specimen had realized that by simply following the railway lines he'd be flying in the right direction. As luck would have it, a signal problem further along the line had caused a severe delay a mile before Harry's embarkation point, so the blackbird had been able to catch up with the long string of fast moving metal boxes, and follow Harry to his destination.

Amplewick Abbey sat perched on a hill overlooking a little orchard and a patchwork of fields. It was a far cry from the council estate with its drug dealers and vandalized cars, and the perfect place from which Harry could commune with God, not to mention his less than happy mother.

Before Harry had got to the bottom of the first page of his letter, there was a shuffling from the corridor outside. The old oak door opened and in stepped a kindly man with white hair and half moon glasses. Father Peter had already had a very long conversation with Harry. He had shown very great interest in Harry's account of the plan to kidnap Roy and the subsequent episode of the geese and the tie, and he had assured Harry that men and women from all walks of life had, since the beginning of time itself, felt the call from the Almighty. This, however, was the first time an eleven-year-old boy had ever walked into the abbey and claimed that he, too, had received this call. The boy had seemed genuinely concerned and had been desperately eager to share his burden.

At first Father Peter had felt a spasm of delight and

wonder that the Lord had sent Harry, a street urchin, to the confines of Amplewick. The boy's story had genuinely intrigued and moved him. But any thought of mentoring Harry and entertaining him in this house of God for any length of time was clearly out of the question. The boy was only eleven years old. It was for this reason that Father Peter had urged Harry to write to his mother. And it was also for this reason that another man standing behind Father Peter now emerged from the shadows.

Harry looked up, deep in thought. "Ah, Harry, I'd like to introduce you to somebody." Father Peter coughed slightly out of embarrassment. He felt he had betrayed the boy's trust, but in reality he had little choice in the matter. "This is Chief Inspector Milner. He'd like to have a little word with you."

At that moment Harry's heart sank. It seemed that every member of the Hodges family had at some point received a visit from the police. And now he'd have to add his own name to that long list.

Harry put down his pen, and as he did, a cold sweat broke out on his forehead. For a split second he could feel his heart pounding like a steam engine in overdrive. What he did next took everyone by surprise, including himself. He opened the latticed window and jumped with the agility of a cat out into the cold, moist air. It was only a short drop to the soft, squidgy, waterlogged grass below. And as his loose clothes absorbed the rain and clung to his skin, he ran like the wind as fast as his tired feet would carry him. He was as free as a bird! No one but no one was going to deny him his freedom - certainly not a member of Her Majesty's constabulary.

Fifty five miles north east of Amplewick Abbey as the crow flies, or for that matter, any bird with stamina, Mr and Mrs Nuttersley were themselves becoming more familiar with the law of the land. In their case, however, it was the law relating to divorce. Apparently, the procedure could in theory be fairly straightforward. But problems and complications could arise if one of the partners were to object to a separation. "In this event," explained Mr Fiddler, "the whole process could become very lengthy, very costly and very messy indeed."

These words came as music to Angela Nuttersley's ears. She would steadfastly object to a divorce no matter how much she really wanted one, in order to simply stop her oaf of a husband getting his own way.

As for Mr Nuttersley, his wife's behaviour seemed to defy any kind of logic. Why on earth would she object to a divorce when she almost certainly had most to gain? As far as he could see, she would get to keep the house and he would have to move out. Indeed, in situations like this most men would have felt a sense of relief that their wives did not want to press ahead with a divorce. But for Stanley Nuttersley, his pride was at stake. He was the boss, or so he liked to believe. And he simply didn't like to be told by anyone what he could or could not do. Besides, there was the other matter of his wife's disgraceful behaviour with another man in this very house. The very thought of it sent a shudder down his spine. How on earth could she deny it when the evidence was as clear as daylight? And how could she hurl such ludicrous accusations back at him that he - of all people - had been unfaithful? How indeed could his pea-brained wife have the bald-faced audacity to create such a ridiculously infantile story about an engagement ring? A ring that did not even exist, except perhaps, in his wife's vivid imagination.

As the letters from the two solicitors landed on the doormat at number 44 Orchard Drive, the atmosphere became more and more difficult for poor Roy to cope with. Mrs Nuttersley had now gone to the trouble of buying several cheap sets of crockery made in the People's Republic of China with which to continue hurling at her husband every morning. The pillow fights too had become a regular feature of daily life in the Nuttersley household, and the dust and feathers that now seemed to permanently waft about the house were beginning to make Roy sneeze. With his cherished bird feeders removed from the trees, Roy could no longer even seek solace from the birdsong in his garden.

As the incessant screaming, bellowing and breaking of crockery began to intensify to unprecedented levels, this terrible state of affairs also began to take its toll on Roy's nerves. Being bullied at school would have seemed like light relief from this nightmare that he now had to live through every day. Amid this terrible chaos he felt he was being subjected to a slow and extremely painful form of torture. In short, the atmosphere was doing rather more than irritate his sensitive nose: it was actually beginning to suffocate him. Though he didn't really fully realize it himself, what hurt most of all was the fact that his parents were so intensely focused on hating each other that they had completely forgotten about him.

Furthermore, his utterly ridiculous parents were now battling through the nights. So he was being deprived of his precious sleep, unable to even escape into the comforting world of his dreams.

And so it was that while that other less than happy child by the name of Harry Hodges had suddenly felt the need to take flight into the fresh and bracing air, Roy too felt this impulsive and instinctive urge to escape for good from the stifling atmosphere of number 44 Orchard Drive.

He didn't really know what it was that attracted him to the huge oak tree that stood so solidly at the bottom of his garden, other than the fact that the birds obviously enjoyed its many sturdy arms and considerable canopy of leaves. But whatever the magnetic force of this magnificent 150-year-old specimen, Roy now found himself clambering slowly but surely up its knotted and weather-beaten trunk.

The task in hand was by all accounts an onerous and perilous one. Some might have gone further and used the word 'insane', seeing that he had begun this impulsive ascent totally unprepared. Nevertheless, Roy was determined to find sanctuary high up in the overhanging branches, well away from the noise and commotion at ground level. And anyway, the tree that had stood for as long as Roy could remember within the frame of his bedroom window was like a dear old friend. Through rain and shine it had stood firm, entrenched and reliable. As far as Roy was concerned there were plenty of unpleasant things in life that could harm him, but the old oak tree that had stood guard outside his bedroom window for all these years certainly wasn't one of them.

Fortunately for Roy the tree was blessed with countless ridges, bumps and crevices for the rubber soles on the undersides of his trainers to get a grip. This said, his ascent was painfully slow. The trunk itself provided him with the most challenging part of his climb. Indeed, most children wouldn't have entertained the idea of attempting to climb it at all, for there were no low branches to seize hold of. Instead, Roy had to make do with knobbly lumps and protrusions on which to secure his footings, and cling to with all ten fingers. It was a most exhausting and at times painful business. But at least the weather conditions here were dry. Had they been anything like the conditions Harry Hodges was now experiencing, Roy's intrepid adventure would have been doomed from the outset, since a wet tree, as everyone knows, becomes incredibly slippery and virtually impossible to climb.

By the time Angela Nuttersley had managed to break

no fewer than forty three pieces of china, and the local police station had received six telephone calls from angry neighbours complaining about the noise, Roy had miraculously managed to reach the first branch of the tree.

From where he now sat he could see the silhouettes of his parents' heads behind the net curtains of the sitting room. The dreadful noise had now ceased due to the presence of the police, and the two parked police cars with their flashing blue lights had caused the net curtains of other houses in the street to twitch incessantly. Roy felt completely embarrassed by his hideous parents. Thank goodness he wasn't down there now. All he wanted to do at this very moment was distance himself as far apart from his parents as was humanly possible. So despite the fact that he was incredibly tired from his efforts, he continued to inch his way up the tree.

Down below the two police constables in the living room at number 44 Orchard Drive had never seen anything quite like it. But then they were new to the job. As the two men paced slowly up and down taking notes in their note-pads the sound of broken china underfoot caused Mr and Mrs Nuttersley to blush.

"So you say this was just a one-off argument. Nothing serious," said the first constable, followed by more crunching of china underfoot.

"Well, I'd say it was a minor disagreement, wouldn't you dear?" said Stanley Nuttersley hesitantly and clearly very embarrassed. Angela Nuttersley made a strange kind of squeaking sound in acknowledgement and looked down at her feet and the crumbs of white china on the carpet. As more notes were copiously taken by the two policemen, Mrs Nuttersley suddenly found her voice.

"Could I get either of you two gentlemen a nice cup of tea?" The younger of the two constables who had distinctive ginger hair and the beginnings of a beard, looked up from his notepad enthusiastically.

"Ooh, that would be very nice. Thank you." His colleague who had precious little in the way of hair and was a little on the chubby side, continued scribbling.

"If you can spare a china cup, that is," he mumbled to himself.

From where Roy now perched he could see gardens that he'd never been able to see before. Most were fairly nondescript, much like his own. Some had brightly coloured children's swings and slides; one or two had greenhouses. Number 48 had a vegetable patch that took up virtually the entire garden. It was a bit like looking down on a model village, he thought to himself.

As Roy observed his surroundings, a number of blackbirds perched on the uppermost branches of the oak tree and watched this latest development with astonishment. Human beings really were the most irritatingly unpredictable of creatures. While the magpies had performed their task with astonishing precision and skill, none of the birds could have foreseen Roy's intrepid response as he now risked life and limb to climb the mighty oak. Then again, neither could they have predicted Mrs Nuttersley's peculiar behaviour when she had so callously removed her son's precious bird feeders and their even more precious contents from the branches of the trees - without rhyme or reason. The blackbirds had intended the battle of the Nuttersleys to provide Roy with the ideal opportunity to restore his bird feeders to their rightful place. But in return, Roy had now planted himself in the tree instead. It was all getting a little out of hand.

As Roy now propped himself up against the trunk, closed his eyes and gently dozed, the blackbirds suddenly came to realize that Roy needed their help more than ever if he was to stay in one piece.

SIXTEEN

The Nest

Dear Mum

I know your annoyed with me for dissapearing like this. Thing is dont get all worked up and dont bovver dad. You know he'll only do his nut. Anyway I'm fine. I'm actually in a monistree. No really. I'm serius. You see I've had these really strange things happen. I know this sounds really weerd right but I actually think I'm being spoken to by...

The letter trailed off at this point leaving a blue smudge where a small globule of ink had inadvertently been smeared across the page by Harry's writing hand.

Father Peter looked up from the desk and peered out of the open window. He could see chief Inspector Milner in the distance, hands on hips. He had stopped running now. Father Peter wasn't surprised in the least. The Chief Inspector was, after all, a portly gentleman.

His mother would have described him politely as well-built. He certainly didn't look like a natural athlete. The child, on the other hand, was lean and lanky and had slipped away into the mist like a hare running to ground. He smiled to himself. Part of him was glad that the boy had escaped. But another part was sad that he hadn't had the chance to speak longer to the child. There was something about him. Something in those brown eyes that had almost touched his soul. He'd seen the look before, of course, in the eyes of those who had suddenly and unexpectedly found the Almighty. Usually though these individuals were middle aged bankers or businessmen who had discovered late in life that there was more to life than making large sums of money. He'd even come across criminals who had wanted to find forgiveness for their crimes through the Lord. But he'd never seen this desperate need to commune with God from one so young as Harry. He looked again at the spidery blue writing on the crisp white sheet of paper. There was no forwarding address at the top of the paper. That was a pity, he thought.

By the time Chief Inspector Milner had given up the chase and had returned to the abbey wheezing and out of breath, Harry was sitting on a bus. He didn't know where it was going, and he didn't particularly care. God was there to guide and protect him. He wasn't going to come to any harm.

If only the blackbirds could have felt the same way about Roy Nuttersley. But of course they couldn't. Well, how could they? There was absolutely nothing to stop the boy from coming to very great harm by falling from the tree as he slept soundly but awkwardly in the crook of one of the oak's many outstretched fingers.

There could be no two ways about it. The blackbirds were going to have to orchestrate something very big indeed this time. They had already proved to themselves that they could achieve the near impossible by getting the Canada geese to co-operate fully and behave in a manner that was unheard of. But what the blackbirds now had in mind was going to take an immense effort on a scale they could not properly comprehend themselves. It was going to involve thousands upon thousands of birds. Birds from communities far and wide. And it would mean that the blackbirds would have to delegate. But time was of the essence.

The two young policemen had finished their interview with the Nuttersleys and were now getting back into their car. The larger of the two men clicked on his driving belt and started the engine. "Well, the name's appropriate don't you think?" he said in a matter of fact way.

"What do you mean?" asked his colleague with the ginger hair.

"The name Nuttersley," his mate replied. "It's perfect. They're a pair of nutters." At this, the two men laughed so hard that it shook their car from side to side.

While the policemen continued to chortle at the joke,

they failed to notice something rather curious. A constant stream of birds was now flying from all directions towards the garden of 44 Orchard Drive. To the human eye this in itself was nothing unusual. But what was strange was this: every single bird among them carried in its beak a piece of twig or branch. And stranger still, as the minutes ticked by, the number of birds seemed to grow. Within half an hour, the numbers had grown so dramatically that the oak tree appeared to be surrounded by a perpetual fuzzy grey halo. Thousands of birds were now coming and going like a huge swarm of bees.

Amidst this extraordinary activity, and despite the constant flapping and beating of wings, Roy slumbered in a very cosy and comfortable world of his own.

It was a glorious day. As he lay in the shade of a chestnut tree, he could see ducks on a lake that reflected the white cotton wool clouds like a mirror. The cherry trees were in full bloom and stood like absurdly large sticks of candyfloss. He was happy. Far happier than he could ever remember. He followed the irregular flight of a white butterfly as it fluttered this way and that and finally settled on a blade of grass close to his hand. The words 'butterfly flutter by' from a distant nursery rhyme or song kept wafting through his head.

And then, as if from nowhere, came the face. It was a giant, beautiful face - even if it was floating upside down. The face looked as happy as he felt. The eyes were vivid blue with distinct specks of yellow, and reminded him of an old paperweight he'd once seen in an antique shop. It had possessed the same vibrant shards of cobalt blue embedded deep within the glassy orb.

The mouth was open, revealing a broad white-toothed smile. And as the smile continued to beam, the long, fair hair that caught flickers of sunlight in their silky strands brushed gently across his cheek and tickled his nose.

Now the face began to descend. The eyes and mouth began to grow. The mouth pursed its lips as they closed in closer and closer. As the lips took up his entire field of vision, the sunlight was being pushed aside altogether. And his world suddenly plummeted into darkness.

He turned at the last moment, for fear of getting crushed by the enormous pair of lips. As he did so, a huge flock of birds took flight from the chestnut tree above him. He could hear the wings beating frantically. Then there came a splintering crack of wood and he felt his whole body fall.

It wasn't a big fall. But the thud onto a springy wooden mattress woke him abruptly.

As he opened his eyes, Roy could feel the morning dew on his face. The mass of leaves and branches against a streaky grey sky slowly came into focus. There were no cotton wool clouds, no cherry trees in full bloom and no looking-glass lakes. Neither was there any face looking down at him benevolently from upon high.

He couldn't remember how long he had been asleep in the tree. But as the real world came flooding back he realized that he was now lying on his back. Surely not. How could this be possible in a tree? He sat up abruptly and took a good look at his surroundings.

He was sitting in what could only be described as an enormous nest, pieced together from countless small twigs. This was ridiculous. How on earth could this be? He was obviously having another one of his peculiar dreams. So he pinched himself hard on his leg to wake himself up. But, of course, this did nothing other than to cause him some considerable pain and leave him with a nasty bruise.

SEVENTEEN

Hitting the Headlines

The clatter of the train as it made its way across the railway bridge made Harry jump in his sleep. The musty smell of the filthy nylon sleeping bag that a young girl with a pierced nose had kindly let him have, brought him to his senses as he now opened his eyes. He'd never attempted to sleep on the pavement before, and it wasn't something he was terribly keen to try again. His whole body was aching like it had never ached before, and the back of his head was feeling very sore from resting on the unforgiving surface of the paving stone. The girl with the pierced nose was now coming over to him with a cardboard cup, her mangy looking mongrel dog trailing behind.

"Here you go sunshine." She handed him a cup of coffee. "How was your first night on the streets of London, then?"

"Alright. Yeah, really, it was ok," he lied, and placed

the cup to his lips. The coffee was lukewarm and far sweeter than he would have liked. He could detect signs of life from the other railway arches as sleeping bags began to slowly move like lazy caterpillars and cardboard boxes began to rustle and topple over, revealing their bleary-eyed owners. So this was what people often called 'cardboard city.'

The girl with the pierced nose was called Debbie, though most of the residents here called her Debs. She'd been sleeping rough for four years and had originally come from a place called Grimsby, which is somewhere in the north, and was clearly why she had an accent.

Most of the people living in the archways were actually pretty young, thought Harry, though some of them had beards and looked older than they really were. None of them, of course, were anywhere near as young as Harry. So he was something of a celebrity and had caused a bit of a stir when he showed up the previous night unannounced and looking lost. Luckily for him, Debbie had taken him under her wing. She'd found him the sleeping bag and managed to find him a spot to sleep.

He hadn't really told her or any of the others very much about himself, other than the area he had come from and the fact that his dad was in prison. He certainly hadn't said anything about the geese and the tie, which he could still feel rolled up in his trouser pocket. In return for these brief details, Harry had received Debbie's entire life story. And some story it was.

Her mother had died ten years ago while giving birth. If this wasn't bad enough, the baby had turned out to have something called 'Down's Syndrome.' Debbie explained that this had meant that the little boy's mental age would never develop beyond the age of eight and that his life expectancy was probably no more than forty years, if he was lucky. As a result, the father had gone to pieces. He'd started drinking whisky and getting drunk, and it wasn't long before he lost his job as an advertising executive in Manchester. Then social services took the baby away and put him into a special home. And that was when her dad started getting violent. The drunken rages got worse and worse, until one day he beat Debbie so hard that he broke her arm and three ribs.

The thing Harry didn't understand was that she didn't seem to hate her father for what he had done. In fact, she hadn't reported him to the police or social services. Instead, she had chosen to run away. And here she was, four years later, living rough with a bunch of other lost souls. His own life seemed quite normal compared to hers. Alright, his dad wasn't up to much and was never there for him, on account of being locked away. And his mum wasn't exactly brilliant. He knew that. But neither of them had ever broken any of his bones.

"Your dad. Did he ever come looking for you?" he

asked, as he finished the last sugary dregs of the coffee.

"Nah. He got ill. Went a bit funny in the head and got admitted to a psychiatric hospital. Bloody horrible place. I wouldn't recommend it." She laughed. Though there was no evidence of laughter in her eyes. "I went to see him, though," she added. "I saw him twice before he died. Trouble is he didn't talk any sense. S'pose he was drugged up to the eyeballs. All he wanted to tell you was that all the terrible things happening in the world were down to him. I mean, what kind of conversation can you have with someone who keeps telling you that?"

Harry didn't know what to say. He shrugged his shoulders and looked down at his shoes. Then her eyes lit up and her tone changed completely.

" 'Ere. Tell you what. Have you ever been to Hampstead Heath?" Harry nodded. He'd heard of it. The scruffy looking dog looked expectantly at its owner at the mere mention of the place. "We could get a bus from here. I've got some money. And anyway you can travel free." With this, she rolled up the smelly nylon sleeping bag, placed it in a brown cardboard box and pushed it into the furthest corner of the archway. "Come on. I'll treat you to an ice cream."

Harry liked Debbie. She may have had a terrible life. But she didn't seem bitter. She was just ordinary and nice. And for this reason he now found himself following this strange looking girl with the pierced nose and scruffy dog.

As they made their way along the street, a gust of

wind blew in their faces and the front page of a newspaper flapped past them like a demented bird and wrapped itself around the back of a street bench that looked out over the River Thames. Harry didn't give the newspaper a second thought.

The slightly fuzzy black and white photograph of a tree seemed innocuous at first glance. But the headline drew you in. 'Bird Boy spotted in world's biggest nest.' It was an unmissable story, or so its author thought.

Robert Jenkins had worked as a junior reporter for The Echo for a year. As a free newspaper that got circulated around the London Underground, The Echo certainly wasn't seen as a serious newspaper at all. But this was one hell of a serious story. And by a strange quirk of fate it had ended up getting into The Echo before any of its more respectable and established competitors.

A rather peculiar man by the even more peculiar name of Duncan Duck had called on Monday morning reporting the sighting of the giant nest in the garden of his eccentric and rather noisy neighbours. He'd spoken at some length to the newspaper's editor who, thinking that the caller was probably just some crank, got one of his juniors to follow it up. That junior reporter happened to be Robert Jenkins.

Until that fateful morning, there had been only two stories he'd written that he thought had any merit. One concerned the issuing of policemen with electric bicycles, and the other was a short piece covering a proposed dustmen strike in North London. Now his luck was about to change.

The editor had laughed. "Look Robert. I've just spoken to this guy called Duncan Duck - but he might just as well be called Donald Duck." It hadn't looked like a particularly promising lead. But like a professional, Robert had gone in search of a story while his boss sat giggling to himself.

46 Orchard Drive had looked like any other late Victorian terraced house and could have been almost anywhere. A black and white tessellated path lead to the front door, either side of which hung two large hanging baskets showing off pink and mauve petunias. Mr Duck, a short man with thinning grey hair, pointed features and a slightly reddish complexion must have been in his forties. He had seemed perfectly normal and not at all peculiar as Robert's boss had seemed to think.

Having almost apologized for calling the newspaper and expressing a certain guilt that some might have accused him of spying on his neighbours' garden, he had lead Robert through the dark and narrow hallway, through a small kitchen and breakfast room and out into daylight at the rear of the house.

The garden was not exceptional. A patch of grass, a couple of overgrown flower beds with manky looking roses and an old greenhouse without any glass in it - all sat in the shadow of the most enormous oak tree which stood at the back of the neighbouring garden. How strange, Robert thought, that such a mighty tree should grow here, in the middle of suburbia when it clearly belonged in a sizeable park or the substantial grounds of a stately home.

Stranger still was the large dark object that seemed to be suspended high up in the branches.

Without even realizing it, Robert had stepped on what news reporters would have described as an almighty scoop of a story. And within four hours, his senior colleagues back at The Echo's dingy offices would be seething that they hadn't been the ones to have uncovered this extraordinary story.

The editor had ripped the first proof of the morning's first edition off the printer and had placed it lovingly on the desk. Having fumbled in a drawer for a fat cigar, which he lit and puffed on extravagantly, he devoured the contents of the first few pages written by the paper's most junior correspondent.

His eyes were drawn to the headline: 'BIRD BOY SPOTTED IN WORLD'S BIGGEST NEST.' It was a terrific line. There was no denying it. The kid had a talent. And he smiled to himself. He'd always had an eye for spotting gifted reporters. Only last year one of his star writers was poached by 'Farmers' Weekly.' He continued to scan down the page in great anticipation.

Today The Echo brings you an exclusive story involving the most extraordinary sighting ever made in a suburban garden anywhere in the world. Thanks to the keen eyes of a Mr Duncan Duck from North London, this newspaper can now reveal to readers a truly unique phenomenon that is so significant; so earth shatteringly dramatic; and so utterly compelling that it will, I'm sure, get itself into every newspaper and onto every television and radio station in the land.

Having stepped into Mr Duncan Duck's back garden I can tell you that what I saw in the upper branches of his neighbours' oak tree quite literally took my breath away. There high up in the branches sat a bird's nest of enormous proportions. It must have been in the region of five or six feet in diameter.

As I strained to see whether I could observe any bird activity in the nest, I can now reveal that what I saw next was not a bird at all, but the small pink face of a young boy, who was peering down at us from the edge of the nest. And it was only then that Mr Duck who was standing next to me exclaimed that the boy in the nest was none other than his neighbours' young son; a boy of eleven years of age by the name of Roy Nuttersley.

The editor couldn't believe it. This stuff was dynamite. He flicked over the page. There were more photographs. A close-up of the nest and another of an odd looking couple. The man was large and balding and his wife was small with a distinctive and not very attractive turned up nose.

The piece continued under a sub heading which

read: 'The family next door.' He took another big puff on his cigar and continued reading.

At Mr Duck's suggestion we knocked on the neighbours next door. Mrs Nuttersley, a petite, middle-aged lady came to the door wearing Marigold gloves, and was in a state of high anxiety. The cause of this distress soon became apparent to us as we were to learn that Mr and Mrs Nuttersley had just been on the telephone to the police in the belief that their son Roy Nuttersley had very suddenly and mysteriously gone missing from the house. Before Mrs Nuttersley could close the front door in our faces, I was able to convey to her that Mr Duck and I had by chance managed to locate her son, and that he was actually rather close to home.

Suffice it to say that it was not very long at all before all four of us were standing at the bottom of the Nuttersleys' garden and peering up into the overhanging branches of the oak tree. But it soon became clear that the boy had no intention of coming down. How the eleven-year-old ever got up there in the first place remains as mysterious to me as the nest itself.

The failure to coax the boy down was beginning to irritate Mrs Nuttersley who now decided it was high time to settle this nonsense once and for all. Her piercing shrieks aimed at her son were quite appalling. But it did at least get a response. Within seconds, a piece of paper came fluttering down from the nest and fell to the grass. I stooped to pick it up. It was a note written clearly with a pencil, and it read as follows:

'Dear Mum and Dad

The birds are my friends.

They have built me this comfortable bed and I intend to stay here until you remove my bird feeders from the shed, and put them back on the trees where they belong.'

There was a pause. Then a larger sheet of paper was released from the nest and gracefully floated around the huge tree trunk before bumping into one of the many outstretched branches and nose-diving to the ground by Mrs Nuttersley's feet. She stooped and picked it up. I could see from where I was standing that it was a letter written in very neat handwriting. But sadly, that is all I can tell you because Mrs Nuttersley swiftly folded it into quarters and stuffed it into her pocket.

The article went on to describe in some length the curious collection of brightly painted bird feeders that were then retrieved from the shed by the Nuttersleys and tied back onto the trees.

The story did not, however, come to a very satisfying conclusion, as Roy Nuttersley seemed unable to descend from his nest for fear of falling the very great distance to the ground. So The Echo simply promised to keep its readers posted as events unfolded.

As you might have guessed, the letter from Roy had been stuffed into Angela Nuttersley's pocket for good reason. She knew instinctively, having read the first few words that this was not something she'd want to share with anyone else.

Now that she was in the privacy of her own home, she carefully unfolded it and scanned the neatly penned lines:

Mum and dad

This isn't just about bird feeders. It's about you and me and the kind of things pairents are ment to do for there children. I mean, when was the last time you asked me how I was feeling and what I thawt of school? And come to think of it, when did eather of you bother to come to open day at school to see my work, or come and watch me in the school play? Even Harry Hodges' mum comes to the school and he hasn't exactly done much that's worth looking at. Thing is, you just don't seem to be interested in me at all. If you are you have a very funny way of showing it. All you seem interested in is screeming at eachother. How do you think that makes me feel? I don't supose you even think about that do you? But it's about time you did. Because I'm fed up with being your son. The truth is I prefer the company of blackbirds to a pair of selfish human beings.

If I ever have kids of my own, which perhaps one day I will, I'd want to make shure that they were happy. And I'd want to help them in any way I could.

Which is why the one thing I'd like more than anything right now is to get away from both of you. Perhaps I could be the world's first child to divorse there pairents. Why not? If adults are allowed to, why shouldn't kids like me be able to? Nothing would give me grater pleshure.

Roy

Angela Nuttersley began to quietly seethe. What a horribly ungrateful and unpleasant little child. She'd never have dared to talk to her own parents in such a disrespectful tone. How dare he? As far as she was concerned, he could stay in that tree until he apologized. He'd be doing them all a favour.

In her anger, she tore the letter into tiny pieces and deposited them unceremoniously into the bin under the kitchen sink.

It wasn't long, of course, before the entire episode of the boy in this larger than life nest reached the eyes and ears of other newspapers and broadcasters. Robert Jenkins' prediction had been quite accurate. For by the time Harry and Debbie had stepped onto the bus to Hampstead Heath, having failed to see the newspaper's famous headline, a very long queue of people and equipment were trying to get into number 44 Orchard Drive.

There were casually dressed men with notebooks and recording machines; men in baseball caps and earphones carrying long poles with strange furry balloons attached; men with cameras of varying size; several blonde women with microphones; young, spotty lads with clapper boards; there were even hairdressers and makeup people.

Orchard Drive had never known anything quite like it.

EIGHTEEN

Celebrity

The sight of the little coloured bird feeders swaying gently once again from the branches of the trees had cheered up Roy no end, not to mention the birds. He'd been up here now for two whole days and had been kept going by the simple meals kindly dropped into the nest by the magpies. These included almost half a chocolate bar with hazelnuts, some wrapped boiled sweets, a couple of small apples and a fair number of strawberries plucked, presumably from Mrs Hinton's impressive kitchen garden at number 48 Orchard Drive. He still couldn't quite believe that the birds had built him such an incredibly large and robust nest.

He hadn't been too sure who the young man in the glasses standing next to Mr Duck, their neighbour, had been. But he had seemed terribly keen to speak to him. Roy, of course, had made it clear that he was having none of this. For a start, he'd been far too tired to engage in any kind of conversation. But more to the point, he wasn't one to shout, and would have had to do just that to get heard.

Instead, Roy had managed to communicate very effectively by writing on scraps of paper and letting them flutter to the ground like little leaves. In this way he had managed to persuade his parents that he had needed to stay put in his nest for a little while longer. He needed to sleep and didn't really want to be disturbed by them, or for that matter, the London Fire Brigade. The young man wearing glasses had, Roy noticed, also been writing notes of his own all along in a little note-pad. How very odd the world seemed to have become.

The fact that Roy had found himself in the very midst of an incredibly newsworthy and extraordinary happening hadn't really sunk in. Yes, it really was out of the ordinary that birds had somehow managed to build him this giant nest. But rather than thinking about the attention this might attract and any possible consequences, he had instead focused his attention on the remarkable ingenuity of the birds and the astonishing speed with which the nest had been constructed. These thoughts had lingered in his head - along with analogies involving hoards of ancient Egyptian labourers building mighty pyramids. And eventually these images and thoughts had become increasingly indistinct and blurred - until the sound of the rustling leaves and the glare of daylight flickering through the branches had faded from his senses.

He was returning now to a familiar spot. It was still warm beneath the chestnut tree and shafts of sunlight were still splashing small, irregular puddles of light across the grass. In the distance, he could make out the figure of a young girl with fair hair and blue eyes. She was wearing a red dress and was coming towards him. As she came closer, her features came into sharper focus. She was certainly attractive, but there was something about her that reminded Roy of himself. The way she walked, the slightly high cheekbones, the splattering of small freckles about the nose and that knowing look in the eye. She was holding something in her right hand: a little parcel tied up with ribbon. Now she was undoing it and dangling it before Roy's very eyes. Coloured wrapping paper with a teddy bear motif was gently peeled away by elegant fingers and a small white box produced. Then and only then was the box opened, and its contents revealed.

There before his nose dangled his precious blue binoculars, their lenses twinkling in the sunlight as the fingers gently swung them this way and that like a pendulum of a clock. Roy lunged forward and tried to snatch them. But his sudden movement abruptly interrupted this vision before him.

Before he knew it the chestnut tree had vanished into thin air and had now been replaced once again by the overhanging branches and leaves of the oak tree. The warmth of the midday sun, too, had evaporated and the air had now become quite chilly. He could feel the texture of the small knitted twigs and branches through his clothes, and there was a distinct background noise - a hubbub of human voices coming from ground level.

He felt very strange indeed and wasn't at all sure how long he had been asleep. The dream had seemed so vivid and so incredibly real that it had completely disorientated him.

As he rubbed his eyes, yawned and peered casually over the edge of the nest, an extraordinary view greeted him.

The little patch of grass below was now home to umpteen individuals - all straining their necks and peering upwards into the branches of the oak tree. They were, Roy realized, trying to catch a glimpse of him. No sooner than he digested this there came a series of loud acknowledgements from the assembled throng.

"There he is."

"Bingo!"

"I see him."

"Camera rolling."

Roy blushed. He wasn't exactly used to this kind of attention. Mind you, he wasn't exactly used to living in a giant nest either.

"Hello. Roy, my name is Kenneth Kerr. I'm a reporter for BBC News. Can I ask you how you came to build this remarkable nest?" The man asking the question was rather stocky and sported red braces. In his right hand was a microphone which he was now thrusting in the direction of the nest.

Before Roy could even begin to collect his thoughts, another voice rang out.

"Hello Roy. My name is Gerald Ward from The Times newspaper. Can you tell me about your fascination with birds?"

Then a young woman with her hair in a bun chipped in with a question Roy couldn't even hear. And within no time at all questions were being fired from all directions. The cacophony of human voices and the ensuing tussle on the ground to occupy the best possible position from which to film and record an interview seemed rather comical to Roy.

The proceedings were being watched with interest from behind a large double-glazed window by Mr and Mrs Nuttersley. They were seated in their living room in two chairs while a tall young man with blonde dyed hair was applying some kind of hideous orange make-up to each of their faces with a large puffy brush.

There was another very elegant and made-up couple sitting on a couch with little silver microphones clipped to their lapels. Hovering around them were several young men in T-shirts who were tampering with a pair of large and very bright lamps. In the middle of the room stood a bored looking teenager with acne and a bulky pair of earphones round his neck. In his hands was the long pole with the large fluffy sausage at the end of it that Roy had noticed in the garden earlier. And next to him was another man in a T-shirt who seemed permanently attached to a camera on a tripod.

"Ok luvvies. I think we're ready to rock and roll. Can we have these two lovely people on the sofa now, David?" A painfully thin man with a small goatee beard and a black polo-necked shirt seemed to be in charge. Stanley and Angela Nuttersley were beckoned to take a seat on their own sofa facing the elegant couple. "Robert and Jennifer my loves, are you alright with the lighting? Not too much glare I hope." The elegant couple on the sofa nodded like a pair of nodding dogs. "Ok. Camera rolling. Quiet please, luvvies."

The show was about to begin.

Mr Eric Tonk wasn't one to watch much television. He certainly didn't have much time for daft chat shows. Yet this afternoon had been a particularly stressful one. Miss Prudence, a stern spinster - who taught maths - had been accused by two sets of parents of not letting their children excuse themselves during lessons to go to the toilet. And this had apparently resulted in much anxiety, not to mention little puddles beneath chairs. Then there had been the episode with the Proctor twins who had managed somehow to lock poor Mr Darweed, the school's new supply teacher, in the stationery cupboard.

So it was with a certain amount of relief that Mr Tonk now relaxed in front of the television with a nice cup of tea. The 'Rob and Jenny Show' wasn't something he'd ever set eyes on before, and though this cheap form of television wasn't at all to his liking, he found himself transfixed by the two strange looking characters being interviewed. He couldn't place them, but there was certainly something about them that seemed very familiar.

The elegant and clearly over-made-up woman interviewer had turned to the small woman with the turned up nose. "Well, Mrs Nuttersley. How does it feel to have a son who seems to have become something of a media star?"

It was the name that finally triggered Eric Tonk's memory. Nuttersley. Of course. How could he forget a name like that? He'd seen the pair of them on several occasions. Mr Nuttersley, he recalled had manned the doughnut stall at one of the school's summer fairs and had somehow managed to demolish most of the sugary buns himself. The son, Roy was instantly forgettable: a mere shadow of a boy. So what on earth was this unlikely couple doing on prime time television? And how could their wimp of a son ever be described as a media star?

Behind Mrs Nuttersley's head was a large tree, which the lens of the camera kept zooming in on in a most irritating fashion. In the branches Mr Tonk could discern a large dark object like a small boat suspended as if by magic. It was all very peculiar. And then, when he was least expecting it, the camera transported the viewer back to the living room and fixed its gaze on the less than attractive face of Stanley Nuttersley in excruciating close-up.

And it was then that Mr Tonk clapped eyes on something that made him sit bolt upright and choke on his cup of tea. Because around Stanley Nuttersley's neck was a very familiar looking tie.

NINETEEN

Heads in the Clouds

By the time the garden at number 44 Orchard Drive had been restored to normality and the last of the assembled reporters and television people had trailed back through the house with all their equipment and paraphernalia, the light in the garden was beginning to fade and Roy's tummy was beginning to rumble. He hadn't been the most cooperative of subjects - he knew that. But then, who would have been in these circumstances? It wasn't as if he'd invited all those terrible people to come over to take pictures and interview him. Now he could see what it must have felt like to be a celebrity or a member of the Royal Family, having this kind of dreadful intrusion into your private life. It was alright for some people, he thought. Some people loved being the centre of attention, but not Roy. He hated having to speak in public at the best of times. The last time he had to do so was during the school's speech competition. He'd chosen to speak about bird watching and Mr Tonk, the headmaster, had fallen asleep.

As his tummy rumbled for the second time that afternoon, Roy's thoughts now turned to food. Although he felt strangely comfortable and secure in his nest, there was no way he could have remained up here for a moment longer without a decent meal inside him. He was starving. Despite the magpies' best efforts, there were no two ways about it: he was going to have to come down.

Now here's a strange thing. While Roy began cautiously to make his slow descent, his two star-struck parents were moving rapidly to a height of almost 20,000 feet.

They were sitting on a small private jet and were at this moment clinking two very large glasses of champagne. The live television interview on the Rob and Jenny Show had been an enormous success, and viewers had tuned into the bizarre interview in such large numbers that the producer of the show had been told to extend the interview and cancel the next one with some minor celebrity.

As if this wasn't enough, the Nuttersleys' sudden claim to fame had taken a new and unexpected twist. Having emerged bleary eyed from their twenty-eight minutes of fame under the heat of the lights, Mr and Mrs Nuttersley had been ushered into the kitchen by the man wearing the black polo-necked shirt. His manner had become even more animated. Apparently,

Mr Matt Clivedon - THE Matt Clivedon, had contacted the station to congratulate the producers of the show.

Matt Clivedon needed little introduction to the tabloid newspapers, or indeed the general public. He was well known as the official spokesman and personal publicity adviser to countless celebrities, including some of the most talented footballers and pop stars - many of whom had at some point in their lives done something to put their glittering careers in jeopardy. Some people called him 'the King of Public Relations.' Others called him such rude names that they cannot possibly be repeated here. The truth of the matter is that Mr Clivedon had become something of a celebrity himself and was, as a result, a very rich man indeed.

Now his office had spoken to the man in the black polo-necked shirt and requested to talk personally to the two stars of the show. And the man in the black polo-necked shirt had handed Stanley Nuttersley his sleek mobile phone. "Go ahead dear," he had insisted. "Just push the green button, and you'll get through to Mr Clivedon's private line. Ooh, I'm so excited for you."

All this had proved a little too difficult for Mr Nuttersley to comprehend. He had mopped the perspiration from his brow and begun to make some apologetic noises about being rather tired when Mrs Nuttersley had kicked him very hard in the shin and intervened. She had taken the phone from her husband and had spoken to the great man herself. And as a result of that polite but short conversation on the phone, the Nuttersleys now found themselves reclining in luxurious leather seats with their feet up, supping expensive champagne while white wispy clouds breezed passed the little windows on either side of them.

Mr Clivedon never did things by half. It was the nature of the man. He'd always been a spoilt individual, ever since a small boy. As an only child with well-to-do parents, he'd always received the best presents, been sent to the best schools and been over-indulged generally. Life had continued for him in much the same vein. Besides, when it came to business he liked to impress. It's why he had invested in his own small fleet of private jets, and also why he liked to dine all his business prospects at Catalans - his favourite restaurant that overlooked that majestically sweeping vista of Lake Geneva in Switzerland.

It's very strange how circumstances and events can completely change the way certain people behave. In the case of Mr and Mrs Nuttersley, it hadn't, of course, been so very long ago that they had been quite literally at each other's throats. But now look at them. A bit of fame and attention in front of the world of television, and a little taste of the good life, and suddenly their problems had disappeared into thin air. They had, it seemed, completely forgotten about the diamond ring and the silk tie: two seemingly simple items that had turned their world upside down. Unfortunately, they had completely forgotten about something else, too. And that something else happened to be their ravenously hungry son.

By the time Roy had finally set foot on the ground, his tummy had rumbled no less than fifteen times. He'd counted them himself. Daylight had all but disappeared now as he made his way to the back door that led to the small kitchen. But try as he might, the handle of the door simply refused to turn. It was no use. It was locked. Roy placed both hands above his eyebrows and peered through the glass panes. There seemed little evidence of life and all the lights in the house appeared to be switched off.

At first, Roy was puzzled by the fact that neither of his parents were at home. They never usually went out during the week, and come to think of it, they hardly ever went out at the weekend either. In the currently hostile atmosphere, with each of them threatening divorce, it was highly unlikely that they would suddenly have gone for a romantic candle-lit dinner for two. And they certainly wouldn't have gone out to see friends, because they didn't have any of those. It just didn't make any sense to Roy. But then nothing was making a great deal of sense anymore.

As he peered though the other windows of the house, into the murky gloom of the lifeless rooms, his puzzlement turned to irritation. How could his parents be so selfish? How could they just disappear like this? Weren't they concerned about the welfare of their son who was stuck high up in the tree? Didn't they love him? And then in a rather detached kind of way he came to the firm conclusion that they obviously didn't. He had suspected as much for a very long time. He couldn't remember when either of his parents had last kissed him; he wasn't even sure that they ever had. His dad had once given him a bear hug - but that was in front of the headmaster, and didn't really mean anything other than to show Mr Tonk that Roy was his son.

Roy couldn't be sure whether it was these thoughts in his head or the empty feeling in his tummy that had finally made him act in such a violent manner. For now he stood there, training shoe in hand, his anger having been unleashed on the French windows. He'd felt this way on a number of previous occasions but had never let himself express his true feelings.

As well as the terrible bird feeder incident, there'd been that time when his parents had taken him to a concert in the park. If memory served him right, the piece that was played was The Four Seasons by Vivaldi. Roy had never heard it before and the sound of all those violins bowing up and down in unison against the rhythmic pulse of the harpsichord had captured his imagination and transported him to another place entirely. So he hadn't even noticed when it began to rain that his parents had decided to go home and leave him on his own. They hadn't even had the decency to leave him with an umbrella. He'd felt pretty angry with them at the time.

Then, of course, there had been the music shop

episode when, on Christmas Eve, he'd visited the local music shop in search of other works by Vivaldi in the small and rarely visited 'Classical Music' section. As it turned out, there'd been nothing at all filed under 'V' other than someone called Vaughan Williams. So he made his way to the front door, only to find that it had been locked. Everyone had gone home early for Christmas without switching off the lights, including a twinkling Christmas tree in the window. Nor had they bothered to check that there weren't any customers lurking in the recesses of the Classical Music section. After all, nobody ever went there. Luckily, there was a telephone on the counter so Roy had used it to call home.

When his mum had heard her son's anxious voice on the other end of the line, all she could do was laugh like a drain. Roy, she chuckled, was a very stupid boy to get himself locked in a shop over Christmas. He'd just have to stay there until Boxing Day and forgo lashings of turkey and Christmas pudding. Had it not been for a passing traffic warden who'd spotted Roy in the window display and had had the good sense to inform the police, Roy may well have spent the whole of Christmas locked in that dreadful shop. Thankfully though, the caretaker who had spare keys and lived above the shop was located swiftly, and Roy was released from his temporary prison within half an hour.

As these all-too-recent memories replayed themselves through in his head, Roy looked down at the mess he'd made. Irregular pieces of smashed window pane now lay at his feet; one of which reflected a perfect full moon that resembled a giant, illuminated Stilton cheese.

Four hundred and sixty miles away, Stanley Nuttersley was staring at an entire plateful of cheeses. As the waiter topped his glass of vintage claret he cut himself a generous wedge of goat's cheese and deposited it on his plate. Before him was the most exquisite view imaginable. The moon shone brightly against the black silhouette of the mountains, and was perfectly mirrored in a still, glass lake.

They were sitting on a large candle-lit veranda that jutted out into the lake itself, and Mr Clivedon had been talking virtually non-stop. As the wine began to do its job, Stanley Nuttersley found that the conversation began to wash over him. Some of the words and phrases had been very clear. But others had been indistinct and muffled. There had been talk of book deals, exclusive interviews to 'lifestyle' publications and media events. It was a very different world to the one of Nuttersley Shirts, but one he could very easily embrace if given half a chance.

Unlike her husband, Mrs Nuttersley had hardly touched any of the food that had been dished up before her. Instead, she had been transfixed by the silver-haired man in the very elegant grey suit. He was clearly a very clever man - very clever indeed. He had already arranged a string of projects for the Nuttersleys to consider - all of which took Mrs Nuttersley's breath away. There were, of course, papers to sign. But all this could apparently wait and be sorted out in due course. She felt very flattered and privileged to be receiving the undivided attention of this incredibly clever man in the nice suit. And she was feeling very light-headed as a result.

Mr Nuttersley, on the other hand, was feeling light-headed for an entirely different reason. The rich sauces, marinades and fine wines were all swishing around inside him to such an extent that he was now feeling extremely happy, without really knowing why. This sudden surge of happiness had got the better of him as he now got up from his seat in an exaggerated fashion, wine glass in hand.

Mr Clivedon was in mid-sentence when Stanley Nuttersley had got up, and Mrs Nuttersley had given her husband the sternest possible look of disapproval. Mr Clivedon was, after all, their host, and a most generous one at that.

"I think at this juncture, this momentous moment in time, I would like to propose a toast..." blurted Stanley Nuttersley in a voice that was rather too loud. "The toast," he continued in a now faltering voice, "is to our remarkable boy, Roy. Our lovely adopted boy Roy without whom we wouldn't receive those very generous cheques from the local authority. And without whom, we wouldn't be here today." Then he did something that he hadn't planned on doing at all. He fell over.

Embarrassing though this scene was for Angela Nuttersley, it did, however, have the effect of bringing her to her senses. This was the first time either she or her husband had admitted in public, or indeed to anyone, that they were foster parents. But more significantly, it was the first time they had spared a thought for that poor adopted boy of theirs in that tree, since this whole fairy tale thing with the media had begun. She hadn't so much as left him a note to say where they had gone. She wasn't even sure if they had had the sense to leave the back door unlocked. And then it hit her like an express train. The worst possible thought anyone in her situation could have entertained. What if the newspapers were to find out? She'd be depicted as the uncaring, money-grabbing monster of a foster mother who had left her adopted son - the real star of the show - stuck in a tree, to fend for himself. Her short career as a media celebrity would be left in tatters. She had only just received a small taster of things to come, thanks to Mr Clivedon.

Angela Nuttersley pushed aside her table napkin and rose from her seat. "I'm sorry Mr Clivedon. I've just remembered that we have some important - very important – business to attend to at home." She offered him a rather limp, outstretched hand, which he attempted to shake.

"But Mrs Nuttersley, can't it wait? What business could be more important than you and your husband's future in the media spotlight?" He paused to wipe his lips on his napkin. "And besides, we haven't even had a peek at the sweets trolley."

It was no good. He was right, of course. They couldn't just leave like that. It would have been a huge insult to their host. And there was every chance that by leaving the restaurant, they'd be blowing their big chance right away. Angela Nuttersley smiled, sat down tentatively and then burst into tears.

As Matt Clivedon offered her his silk handkerchief with which to dab her streaming eyes, a large red face appeared from behind the table at the far end, as if emerging from the depths of Lake Geneva itself. "I do apologize most profusely for that most unfortunate mishap," croaked its owner. Stanley Nuttersley plonked himself ungainly back into his chair.

Mr Clivedon had been used to temperamental clients in the past, but he had to admit that he'd never before had clients quite as odd as the two specimens before him.

TWENTY

Homing Instincts

It was the whimpering of the dog that had woken her, and not for once the rattling of the early morning train above. Debbie slowly forced her sleep-encrusted eyes open. It was still dark: ridiculously dark. Why had the dog woken her at such an unearthly hour? He couldn't be hungry surely – not after all those chips he'd polished off the previous night. But the reason for the dog's behaviour soon became apparent. In the corner of the railway arch the blue sleeping bag lay lifeless, flat and empty. Harry had gone.

If she was honest with herself, she knew deep down that Harry wasn't going to stay. And a part of her was pleased that he was no longer sleeping under a railway arch. It was no place for an eleven-year-old: she knew that. But another part of her felt desperately sad. She'd grown fond of the boy in a mothering kind of way. She'd never had the opportunity to look after a kid before, and had found that it was something she was actually pretty good at. She was able to have a positive influence - even teach the boy stuff. It was refreshing, but more than anything it was company. And she was going to miss that.

For his part, Harry was going to miss Debbie too. But sleeping on the street wasn't something he was going to repeat so quickly. Not that he got any sleep of course. He felt exhausted, filthy and cold. And he was pretty sure that he didn't smell too nice either. All he wanted in the world was a nice warm bath followed by a nice warm bed.

He'd been on the bus for ten minutes. It was one of those all-night ones. He'd never been on one of those before. As he sat there on the top deck enjoying the warmth of the heating system, he felt pangs of guilt similar to the ones he felt after the geese episode. He should have left Debbie a note. She'd been a good mate. She'd spoilt him and he'd had fun with her. Besides, she'd listened to what he had to say. And he'd told her everything. Everything about Roy, the kidnapping plan, the geese and the tie. And unlike Father Peter, she had just laughed and made light of it. She'd said that he'd made a 'mountain out of a molehill.' He didn't know what that meant but it sounded good. She'd said that life was full of weird stuff, and none of it was down to God because as far as she could tell, God didn't exist. If he did exist, she reckoned her mum wouldn't have died, her dad wouldn't have gone funny in the head, and she wouldn't be living on the streets. He supposed she was right: she was right about most things. And if she was, then he had nothing to worry about. So that, at least, was reassuring.

The heat and motion of the bus were now making him feel content and drowsy, and before he knew it he had slumbered into the deepest of sleeps.

Roy too was feeling distinctly more human now. He'd demolished four pieces of cheese on toast and was washing it down with a large mug of hot chocolate. He may have felt better in a physical sense but he was feeling decidedly miserable and lonely. It was hardly surprising really. His parents hadn't just disappeared mysteriously without any explanation; they'd gone and locked him out of the house.

He'd show them! He'd finish all the biscuits in his mum's biscuit barrel and make crumbs all over her precious carpet. Then he'd pour the contents of his dad's prized bottles of vintage wine down the plughole. And then he was going to leave home for good, and return to his nest. This was Roy's plan.

Harry, on the other hand, didn't have much of a plan, other than to return home and get cleaned up. He hadn't thought about how he'd handle his mum's anger. She was bound to explode big time. She always did over the smallest things. And his disappearance could hardly be classed as a 'small thing.' Oh well. He'd think of something he supposed. As he rubbed his eyes and stepped off the bus, the silhouette of the council estate came into view, and Harry suddenly realized that there was another significant problem to overcome. It was four in the morning and he didn't even have the front door keys.

It was only now that Harry had gone that Debbie had given any thought to her little brother with Down's Syndrome. She hadn't thought about him for years. Well, you don't want to dwell on the sad things in life, do you? His name was David and he was eight years younger than her, so he wouldn't be much older than Harry - assuming, of course that he was still alive. She didn't suppose she'd recognize him now though. She wondered what kind of life he was leading, and whether he was happy. She hoped he was happy - a lot happier than her. There was, she thought, a good chance that he would be, because she'd read somewhere that people with Down's Syndrome can and do lead happy and fulfilling lives. In some ways, it was probably just as well he only had a limited understanding of the world. If she had been blissfully unaware of all the bad stuff going on in her life and around her, she'd probably be a happier person for it. She tried to picture David's face, but all she could see was Harry smiling with a blob of ice cream on his nose. The image brought a smile to her own face as she now rolled over and hugged the dog who had nuzzled up to her sleeping bag. It was getting distinctly cold and there was something of a gale kicking up and howling through the trees and across the Thames.

By the time Harry had reached the estate, the wind had begun to cut through him like an ice-cold knife. As he thrust his hands deep into his pockets and bolted the last few hundred yards up the steps, a sudden gust of wind caught a couple of empty milk bottles and threw them against the brick wall of the balcony outside his own front door.

The smash of glass had caused one of the lights inside the flat to come on, and as Harry climbed the last few steps, the front door opened.

Harry froze in the shadow.

His mother wearing his dad's old dressing gown was standing in the doorway backlit by the hall light. The two of them just stood there looking at each other for what seemed like eternity, neither of them saying a word. There was nothing to say. And then his mum just stepped forward and took him in her arms and hugged him really hard. Then, before she took her son inside, she did something she had never done before: she kissed the top of his head tenderly, as if he was the most precious thing in the world, which, of course, he was.

TWENTY ONE

A New Chapter

Despite the icy wind and pitch-black darkness, Roy had managed to climb back into his nest. It was by no means an easy task, but he had to admit that he'd found it considerably easier second time round and had somehow managed to remember exactly where the footholds were on the trunk. Naturally, the fact that he had already climbed the tree once had also given him a great deal of extra confidence. So much so that he was now wearing his old and quite heavy duffel coat and carrying a small knapsack over his shoulder.

As he lay on his back gazing up at the moon and listening to the gale howling through the branches, Roy felt strangely more relaxed and less angry with his parents. He hadn't failed to notice on the previous evening that countless blackbirds had perched high up above him, motionless with their little heads tucked into their wing feathers. It was remarkable how they could go to sleep like that for hours on end and not lose their balance. Roy had read about it in the library. Apparently, when birds relaxed, their little claws automatically locked tight like a vice around the branch they were sitting on. So long as they remained asleep, they simply couldn't fall. Now there were considerably fewer of them in the tree, since the gale was causing the branches to sway quite dramatically. But there were still one or two who seemed determined to stay put, come what may.

Roy closed his eyes, buttoned the top toggle of his duffel coat and snuggled into the thick woollen layer. If blackbirds could weather the storm, so could he. He wanted to return to the world of his dreams: to the shady spot beneath the chestnut tree. He longed to catch another glimpse of the girl with fair hair and blue eyes. He had always been a heavy sleeper, which had drawbacks when it came to getting up for school during the week. But on this occasion it was just as well, for it wouldn't be long before the gale would turn very nasty indeed.

In fact, had Roy possessed a television set in his nest, which of course he didn't, he'd have been able to see the weather forecast presented by a little man in a bow tie and a nasty checked jacket who was at this very moment warning viewers of 'an impending hurricane.' This was apparently down to global warming.

The hurricane was actually travelling at a speed of almost 100 miles per hour and was making its way from the North Atlantic. Soon it would be sweeping across the country from northern England and creating mayhem in its wake. Chimney pots and roof tiles would be torn from rooftops, panes of glass sucked from greenhouses and conservatories, and trees directly in its path would buckle and crash to the ground.

By the time this awesome force of nature was to make its presence felt in Orchard Drive, Roy would be blissfully unaware of the screaming wind and the cracking of boughs around him. He'd be oblivious to the terrible force and magnitude of the hurricane, and he certainly wouldn't feel the movement of the nest as it was ripped from the branches and hurled like an Olympic discus into the night sky.

The nest, being large and flat was, it seemed, perfectly shaped to harness the force of nature in much the same way as a surfboard could be made to ride the waves of the sea. Only in this instance, the surfer in question would have no control over his mode of transport since he'd be sleeping like a log. And so it was that while Roy slept the deepest of sleeps, this sturdy flying saucer made from twigs would carry him some considerable distance across the starlit sky.

Roy, of course, was in his favourite place beneath the chestnut tree. There were no golden shafts of sunlight now though. In fact, there was a terrible wind howling through the branches above him and he was feeling rather cold. The grey, stormy sky was having the effect of making everything else around him look grey and miserable too. Roy no longer had the feeling that he wanted to be here at all. It was odd. It wasn't as if he felt this way because it was cold and miserable and that the wind was making a terrible racket in his ears. It was for some other reason altogether. A reason that Roy simply couldn't put his finger on. But the overwhelming sense of sadness he was now feeling was very real and intense.

Before he had a chance to think too hard why it was he felt this way, Roy's ears were greeted with an unexpected sound: that of an approaching vehicle, and as he turned, a white van rolled past before his eyes. As it did so, he couldn't help noticing that the tail of the van housed a window out of which stared a face. It was the face of the young girl with the blue eyes. But her eyes were no longer full of laughter. Instead they were wet and glistening from tears.

Why was she in the van? Where was she going? Why was she crying? And why had he felt so sad before he'd even set eyes on the girl in the van? It was as if he had known all along that this was going to happen. But of course he hadn't. It was all getting far too confusing for poor Roy. His mind began to race.

Before he could arrive at any meaningful conclusion, he was put out of his misery by an incredibly violent thump. The thump was accompanied by the deafening crack of splintering wood and a sharp thwack as Roy felt himself being thrown through the air. The final sensation was not at all pleasant and was rather like being thumped hard in the tummy with something very large but not especially hard.

It was the most brutal way to have been woken from a dream. But now as his senses were able to get some kind of grasp of reality he could tell that he was no longer in his nest. He was in fact lying face down on a large and slightly moist haystack. Above him his nest hung in sorry tatters from the emaciated branches of a half dead tree cloaked in ivy.

The gale had passed now and the early morning light gave the landscape around him a distinctly blue and peaceful tinge. Roy had no idea where he was and how he had managed to get here. What he did know was that his ribs were feeling very sore and he was hungry. As he got to his feet, he took in the scene around him while brushing pieces of straw from his coat.

From the top of the haystack he could see that he was in the middle of a field dotted with numerous haystacks. Surrounding this field were others of varying size and shade - all separated by low lying hedges: an enormous patchwork quilt spread out across the undulating vista as far as the eye could see. The view was pretty, but oddly, it was also a little familiar. Perhaps he'd seen it on television or in his geography textbook at school. In the distant fields there were a few sheep roaming, but otherwise there was very little sign of life.

Without really knowing in which direction to head, Roy simply scrambled down the haystack and set off in the direction that took his fancy. Before long he found himself on a footpath of sorts and carried on without a care in the world.

The cottage first appeared as a white speck nestling between the fold of two distant fields. The path seemed to be heading towards it so he continued with a sense of purpose. It must have taken at least half an hour to reach. When he finally did, Roy suddenly stopped in his tracks, and he felt the hairs on the back of his neck stand on end. Because there, no more than a few hundred yards behind the cottage, lay a small glass-like lake with ducks. There were cherry trees, too. But before he could just put this down to some kind of extraordinary coincidence, his eyes were drawn like two magnets to a small picnic table. It stood beneath the graceful arms of a chestnut tree. The very same chestnut tree under which Roy had first seen the girl with the blue eyes, the girl in his recurring dream.

Roy stood transfixed by the vision before him. It was some little while before he could bring himself to inspect the tree at closer quarters. When he did, he ran his fingers across the textured grain of the trunk and sat beneath the canopy as he had in his dreams. Then for some inexplicable reason he picked himself up and ran towards the little whitewashed cottage with its grey, slate roof. His ribs may have hurt, but he simply didn't care.

Without a second thought he pushed the front door, which opened easily enough and stepped into the half-light of its cosy interior.

It was a simple country cottage with little in the way of natural light, due to its small windows. The room he was standing in was clearly the kitchen since there was an old fashioned looking stove in one corner and a butler sink to the side. In the other corner was a broom cupboard and next to this stood a door. Roy stepped across the stone floor and opened it. On the other side of the door was a little sitting room. Here there was a fireplace with orange glowing coals, and to one side of the fire sat the one person he knew would be here.

She had her back to him and was obviously asleep. Roy pensively tiptoed around the chair and fixed his eyes on its occupant.

She was older than the girl in his dreams, and her hair colouring was a little darker too. In fact, she wasn't really a girl at all. But she was the same person, of that there could be little doubt.

While the coals in the grate gently crackled, he stood gazing at her in the way that children often watch small babies asleep in their cots, without wishing to disturb them. And then, of course, his presence was sensed and the woman opened her eyes. The same blue eyes that Roy had seen so vividly in his dreams. The eyes studied him closely and then filled with tears.

For all these years she had thought of nothing other than her own flesh and blood. She couldn't tell how many years it must have been. Maths wasn't one of her strong points. Nor was reading or any other serious subject come to that. But she was good at cooking and basket weaving, which she got paid for. No one could deny that. And she was a good person. So why should a good person have their right to be a mother taken away from them? She had prayed every night that Roy would come back to her. The thing was, nobody understood her. But then, how could they? How could anyone ever understand what it felt like to have your own baby taken away from you just because you couldn't do sums and spell your own name? That wasn't such an awful crime, was it? The world was a complicated place. She knew that. But what everyone else in this complicated world didn't know was that she had feelings, too. And sometimes those feelings could become so painful that you didn't want to carry on. She looked into his blue eyes. It was Roy alright. She wouldn't have mistaken him in a million years. So even people like her: people with so-called 'issues,' 'problems' and 'learning difficulties,' could be rewarded by their efforts and have their prayers answered.

She hugged her boy with all her might and uttered his name gently over and over again. Roy felt her salty tears trickle down the side of his neck, but try as he might, he couldn't bring himself to utter the simplest of sounds. He was overwhelmed by his emotions, stifled by his own feelings which were both happy and sad. He had never known this kind of raw affection, and no words or utterances could possibly have expressed how he felt.

High above the cottage, however, a flock of five thousand blackbirds were able to speak most eloquently on Roy's behalf. They hovered momentarily above the slate roof and sang like they had never sung before. And as they did so, the morning sun cast its shafts over the gentle hills, and daylight seeped through the small windows of the cottage, throwing fleeting shadows of birds dancing in flight across the cold, stone floor.

The End

Acknowledgements

As a newcomer to the world of writing fiction, I should firstly like to thank two people in particular for their encouragement and words of wisdom. Hugh Salmon, co-founder of www.lovereading.co.uk was kind enough to praise my tatty manuscript from the off, and urged me to get it into print. And George Layton, the actor, author and screenwriter was incredibly generous with his time - offering to read my manuscript, and subsequently pointing out the need for an embellishment in the storyline; a perceptive observation that led me to develop a particularly memorable scene in chapter 19. I should also like to thank my good friend the photographer, John Mac for producing an exquisite cover and promotional film for the book, along with Red Button Publishing for doing an excellent job on the typesetting of this edition. Last but by no means least, I'd like to thank my wife and kids for their unflinching support, without which none of these words would have made it onto paper.

Printed in Great Britain
by Amazon

74263852R00109